Death on the Diversion

Also by Patricia McLinn

Secret Sleuth series

Death on the Diversion

Death on Torrid Avenue

Death on Beguiling Way

Death on Covert Circle

Caught Dead in Wyoming Series

Sign Off

Left Hanging

Shoot First

Last Ditch

Look Live

Back Story

Cold Open

Hot Roll

Reaction Shot

Mystery with romance

Proof of Innocence

Price of Innocence

Ride the River: Rodeo Knights

Death on the Diversion

Secret Sleuth, Book 1

Patricia McLinn

Dear Readers: If you encounter typos or errors in this book, please send them to me at Patricia@patriciamclinn.com. Even with many layers of editing, mistakes can slip through, alas. But, together, we can eradicate the nasty nuisances. Thank you! — Patricia McLinn

PROLOGUE

CALL ME SHEILA M.

At this moment, I'm walking circuits on the deck of a cruise ship called the Diversion on its two-week repositioning cruise from Barcelona, Spain to Tampa, Florida. I'm being passed by runners, joggers, and faster walkers. That's all fine with me. I'm enjoying the air and the sun and the peace.

I'm watching people. Eavesdropping a little.

Thinking about the past fifteen years.

Wondering about the next fifty-plus.

I'm about to find a dead body.

But that's getting ahead of the story.

Sheila M. is not the name you might know me by if you read a certain kind of book, listen to a certain kind of interview, watch a certain kind of TV talk show. Or if you were not in a cave protected from all news about blockbusters—book and movie—fifteen years ago.

But Sheila Mackey is the name I'll use in the life this story leads to. Might as well start now.

Besides, I'm leaving behind that other person, the one with the name you might know.

This moment in time I'm taking you to occurred while I was transitioning to my current circumstances and transitioning from the life I'd lived the previous fifteen years. Contrary to what most might guess, that past is the boring part. So, let's get it out of the way.

Back when I was finishing college, I said yes to a job offer.

No big deal, right? It's what lucky graduates do after college. My friends said yes to job offers with tech firms, oil companies, charity foundations, and the FBI, among other things.

I said yes to my great-aunt.

At that point, Aunt Kit—we left off the *great* most of the time— had been a working fiction author for more than thirty years after a brief stint in journalism. She'd written mysteries, science fiction, romance, horror, westerns, and more. She'd written under her name and five pen names. She'd ghost-written for celebrities. She'd support- ed herself with her writing all through those years. Nothing grand, just, as she would say, a working stiff mid-list author.

Then she wrote *Abandon All*.

A departure for her. A book that bridged the commercial and the literary. A book with huge potential.

A book no one in publishing would buy from her.

That's not a proven fact, since she never submitted it to any pub- lishers. It was a conclusion she drew from decades of experience in the business.

For this book to reach its potential, she told me during that strang- est of job interviews, it needed to have been written by a young, attractive woman from the Midwest. Which she was not. At least not any longer.

"But *you* are, Sheila. Young, very attractive, from the Midwest, with brains and freshness. You are perfect to be the author of *Abandon All*."

I'd laughed. "I can't be perfect to be its author, because I didn't write it. I've always wanted to write, but I haven't actually written anything. Much less a novel. Specifically, one called *Abandon All*."

"You don't need to write it, because I have. You need to be its public face—face, figure, and voice. I am, essentially, your ghostwriter. I'll provide what you need for the public role and pay you."

There was a good deal more discussion, but the bottom line is I said yes. I was, after all, an English major with an undergraduate degree and no idea what to do next. If *Abandon All* drew interest from publishers, Aunt Kit would front the money for a trip to New York for both of us.

It did.

She did.

There was an auction for the right to publish the book—that's where publishers bid against each other, though there's no fast-talking auctioneer with a gavel—that set my head spinning.

Abandon All was not just a hit, it was a phenomenon, a cultural icon. The day an interviewer called it this century's *To Kill a Mockingbird*, I thought I'd faint right there on live TV.

The movie was even bigger.

In less than a year, Aunt Kit and I moved into a brownstone on the Upper West Side. She paid for it outright.

Over the rest of the fifteen years, my name, face, and voice remained the public front for Aunt Kit's writing. She wrote eight more books for that persona—me. (Sometimes I forgot it was me and thought of that person as separate.) None reached the Olympian heights of *Abandon All*, but they did fine financially. She paid me thirty-five percent of the author's earnings—saying I did more for those books than the agent, who took twenty percent off the top—plus provided my housing, "author" clothing, food, and transportation.

Perhaps more important, she invested my money. Aunt Kit was careful and shrewd.

She also wrote another twenty-five books in her old genres for "fun" and published them independently. That income was all hers, as it should be. Though she argued with me, focusing on the brainstorming I'd done with her, particularly for the mysteries. She would set up a scenario, then we'd sit together and brainstorm how her character would approach figuring out whodunit.

I argued back that it was fun.

She'd snorted. "Might be fun. It's still work. You're good at characterization and you, especially, have an excellent grasp of how a character would follow clues. You—"

"Because I'm nosy."

"—should be writing yourself. Nosiness is a great trait for a writer."

"Maybe I will write someday."

Another snort, conveying she knew I didn't believe it. She stuck to her point. "In the meantime, I should pay you for your input."

"No. You pay me more than enough for the other."

She stopped arguing, which meant she planned to see I got that money one way or another.

For the "job" for which I did accept compensation, I did appearances, I spoke at literary events, I walked red carpets, I offered writing advice (culled from Aunt Kit), I was videoed and photographed, and I gave interviews.

No one except the two of us, my parents, and siblings knew I wasn't writing the books. To the outside world, I was offering a home to my aging relative, instead of vice versa.

I'd said yes on a lark.

I ended up being tied to a lie.

For fifteen years.

Could I have left? Should I have left? Certainly. Probably. I didn't. So, what's the use of thinking about it? (An Aunt Kit-ism: You can't change the past.)

Then, six months ago, she said she was retiring.

She might continue writing her fun books as she felt like it, but she was tired of the literary pretentions *Abandon All* taught readers and critics to expect when my name was on a cover. She probably also was tired of hearing the author should write another *Abandon All*. She said one should be enough.

She—she was always kind enough to say *we*—had earned enough and under her guidance we were both set for life. Plus, there'd be ongoing royalties.

She bought a place on the beach in the Outer Banks of North Carolina, which I was invited to visit at any time, but was not to be my home.

She was pushing me out of the nest.

This cruise was a cushion for my landing and Aunt Kit's idea for a lowkey farewell performance as the name you'd probably recognize, though no one else knew it was a finale.

One good thing I'd done at the start, more out of a kind of shyness than smarts, was to use one of my middle names and my mother's maiden name—also Kit's last name—on the books. That left me other parts of my legal name to use in my new life. Not wanting to return completely to my pre-*Abandon All* name, I decided on Sheila Mackey, taken from pieces of other family names.

As for the "author" of *Abandon All*... Time would pass without a new release. If enough questions were asked, a statement would be made about retirement and the desire for privacy. The word *recluse* might pop up. If it added to the sales of the existing books, we wouldn't complain.

So that was me, walking around the ship, in mid-air after the push out of the nest.

Would I fly? Would I crash?

Step one: Figure out how to flap these things sticking out at my sides.

No, I take that back.

Step one: Figure out how I got blood on my finger from touching the woman wrapped up in the pool towels.

How's that for a start on a new life?

Bloody woman and I'm about to become a sleuth with a secret identity.

CHAPTER ONE

"I COULD KILL her."

It all started when those words floated up to us as Petronella and I walked onto the cruise ship in Barcelona in early November, ten days before I found the woman who'd stopped breathing.

I need to explain about Petronella. Possibly about me, a single woman in her mid-thirties, taking a two-week transatlantic cruise, too.

Aunt Kit explains both.

Petronella was the daughter of Kit's long-dead fiancé's cousin from his mother's side. Welcome to Kit's world. I got to the point where I referred to everyone as Kit's relative. It made it easier. Though it did confuse our Guatemalan housekeeper at the brownstone when I introduced *her* as Kit's relative to a visiting acquaintance.

Aunt Kit took me on my first cruise shortly after the *Abandon All* auction and then at least once a year since. Always transatlantic, always from Europe back to the United States, as they moved the ships into place for winter cruises to the Caribbean. (Yes, you can take more than one a year that fit those requirements…with planning.)

"They're long. They're frequently out of range of the internet. Low percentage of the passengers attempt to stay as drunk as possible for the duration. You gain an hour about every two and a half days," was her explanation for choosing those cruises.

I agreed with each point. Also, the author of *Abandon All* went largely unnoticed on these cruises. A major bonus.

Kit booked this cruise as my transition, and here I was.

But I lied.

Or, more accurately, I was an unreliable narrator in saying it started when Petronella and I boarded the ship. (And notice I didn't mention Aunt Kit boarding the ship. Yes, she abandoned me on this trip. More—much more—on that later.)

It—the dead woman in the deck chair—started *well* before I found her body.

If I were Sam Spade, I'd say it started when the dame walked onto the ship. And that would be true—from my POV. POV is author talk for point of view—which character is steering the bus for that part of the story, so the reader experiences it through his or her mind and senses.

From the point of view of the woman dead in the deck chair, it started much earlier. At some point in her life when seeds took root that grew into someone killing her.

For me, it started with that voice carried on an air current up the boxy zigzag of the gangplank.

"I could kill her."

I looked over the railing to the series of switchback ramps below us that created easygoing boarding for the Diversion. Fellow passengers strung out behind us among the early arrivals that Sunday afternoon. A daisy chain of gray heads interspersed with determinedly *not* gray heads and sunhats, male and female.

No telling where the words came from. Not even a hundred percent a woman spoke them. More like sixty percent. Maybe fifty-five.

And what did it matter? We've all said the same thing how many times in our lives?

Except something in the voice made me look.

Then I forgot about it, because it was our turn to be welcomed onto the Diversion.

In the background stood a young woman dressed in a crisp white shirt with insignia and nametag over navy slacks, holding balloons and a sign bearing Petronella's name.

I nudged Petronella with a smile. "Look."

She clasped a hand to her throat. "Oh, God. Someone's died."

"I doubt they'd carry yellow and red balloons to notify you of a death."

The tears in her eyes apparently blocked her hearing, because she didn't relinquish her panicked horror as I dragged her toward the smiling young crew member.

"This is Petronella," I told her.

The young woman's smile flickered, but she handed an envelope and the red balloon to Petronella. "Hope you enjoy your treat, miss." She looked at me more shyly. "And I believe this is for you? We were asked not to use your name publicly because… because of who you are."

Or were.

I didn't say that aloud. I thanked her for both of us, took the envelope and yellow balloon, and dragged Petronella out of the mainstream of boarding passengers.

I ripped my envelope open. She shook, tears sliding down.

"It's from Kit," I said brightly.

"Oh, my God. Kit's dead!"

"Not unless she's writing to us from heaven." Or elsewhere. I loved Kit dearly, but I didn't see her getting a direct ticket through the pearly gates. "She's booked manicures for us—" I checked the clock. "—in ten minutes. To get us in the mood and pass some of the time before we can settle in our cabins."

When you embark on a cruise, your main luggage is whisked away to appear outside your cabin door at some point in the future. All very nice, but that point in the future frequently ends up being unpredictable.

Kit taught me to carry a go-bag to make waiting for the magic more pleasurable.

The go-bag held all the necessities for several hours of relaxation, from sunscreen and sunglasses to reading material and headphones to a few munchies and a thermos of cold water Petronella insisted on filling for me. Today wasn't hot, but quite warm in the sun.

November on a cruise from eastern Spain to Gulf Course, Florida can be variable. But it's not November in the Midwest, where I grew up, or Manhattan, where I'd spent the past fifteen years.

In those places you're more likely to need gloves, hats, scarves, boots, and hot chocolate than sunscreen, sunglasses, and cold water.

But my summery-here supplies were on hold, thanks to Kit arranging for these manicures.

"Are you sure? Maybe my envelope isn't the same..."

Petronella brought out the worst in me. I so wanted to say, *Yeah, you're right. Kit sent me a balloon and a manicure, but you she sent a balloon and the news that one of your nearest and dearest has died.*

With more determination than grace, I said, "I'm sure. Open your envelope."

While she did, I attached both our balloons to a nearby railing—railings are nearby almost everywhere on a cruise ship.

With still-shaking hands she removed the card.

"Oh. It's for a manicure," she said in astonishment.

CHAPTER TWO

"DID YOU HEAR? The she-devil is onboard."

"*No.*"

"Shh." The whispered order from the spa receptionist to her coworker was banished with a perfect, professional smile. "May I help you?"

She-devil? Had I heard correctly? I wasn't supposed to have heard. It seemed such an unlikely word, especially in the bright and shiny spa of the Diversion.

"I'm Sheila Mackey—"

"I will do your nails, miss." The mahogany-skinned young woman who'd exhaled that distressed *No* smiled at me.

I smiled back. "—and this is Petronella—"

"Yes, ma'am," said the receptionist. "We have *detailed* instructions. Everything has been spelled out *precisely*. Right this way, Miss Petronella."

"Oh, no, I couldn't possibly. This is too much." Petronella had protested all the way to the spa—up several decks—and wasn't done yet. "I shouldn't..."

"This way," the receptionist kept repeating, leading us past an open area to our left with a hallway straight ahead. The receptionist gestured to the hallway's first door. "Right here for you."

Petronella put on the brakes. "Oh, no. I couldn't possibly."

Another smiling young woman came out of the room and told Petronella, "The instructions specifically said you were to have a private room."

This smiling young woman also wore the uniform of the ship's spa. She had an Eastern European accent and a firm hold on Petronella's arm.

Were Kit's reasons for this arrangement to spare me? Or more Machiavellian?

At the moment it was moot. Petronella wasn't budging.

"Oh, no, no. I couldn't possibly…"

If you mentioned Petronella—known throughout Kit's extended and far-flung web as *Poor Petronella*—to anyone in my corner of the family, they instantly mimicked, "Oh, no, I couldn't possibly…" Sometimes at the most inopportune moments.

You'd be saying, "I walked up to the casket beside Poor Petronella and—" You'd be interrupted by a chorus of "Oh, no, I couldn't possibly…" instantly followed by chuckles.

According to Kit, this distant relative of her long-dead fiancé had been *Poor Petronella* since she was old enough to display a personality, which came later than most kids.

If there was a mishap floating around, Petronella reached out and grabbed it like the last life jacket on the Titanic—sorry, not a good image when I'm talking about cruising. But it fits.

Her latest misfortune was getting divorced by the husband who'd been abusing her mentally, physically, emotionally, and financially since before they were married. Yes, *before* and she still married him.

You should hear Aunt Kit on *that* topic.

Then how was the divorce a misfortune, you might ask. You and me both. To Petronella, however, it was a tragedy of epic proportions.

Her kids, who loved her for reasons beyond explanation but with the sane caveat of living in distant time zones, begged Aunt Kit to beg me to help her.

They'd thought I would pay for the cruise, while Kit would have soulful, reasonable talks with Petronella.

Instead, Kit paid for the cruise, then bailed on both of us.

"You must go in the room to be happy and for your giver to be happy," said the young woman who'd been talking with the receptionist when we arrived and said she'd do my nails. South African accent, possibly with English not her native language. Her nametag read Imka.

Between Petronella's protests, she put one arm across Petronella's back and the other on her forearm and simply walked forward, scooping along the recalcitrant client. In less time than I could have imagined, Petronella was in the room off the hallway and the door closed.

"Do not worry. Your relative will be very fine."

"I'm not worried about that. I am a little worried about your colleague and I'm wondering if I could learn that move."

She slanted a look at me, apparently found me trustworthy, and said in a low voice, "I learned helping with the old ones at home. They don't always want to go where it's best for them to go. But it's not respectful to pick them up and put them like a child."

"Very true." Though Petronella wasn't that old. Chronologically.

Imka waved me to an open area with floor-to-ceiling windows angled out at the top. If you wanted to look almost directly below, you could by leaning out. But why would you want to?

Two chairs in white leather—crossbred from recliners and airline pilot seats—offered the best views of the windows, blow-out stations, hair dryer chairs, and the hallway, depending on which way you swiveled.

One was occupied by a woman around Aunt Kit's age. She had mostly gray hair, with dark brown at the back. Laugh lines waited for employment at the corners of her mouth and eyes. They flickered when she smiled, polite but not intrusive, as I was directed to the other chair.

"I'm afraid you have a remedial case here," I told Imka.

I'm not the best about getting regular manicures—something the publicist reminded me before each TV appearance—but never far enough ahead of time for me to actually *get* a manicure. Just enough to make me feel insecure about my long, too often raggedy nails.

Imka smiled broadly, rounding her cheeks becomingly. "We will fix you."

I wished that were true, since that promise seemed to cover more than nails.

The older woman met my gaze and her laugh lines deepened.

I said hello. She did the same. She introduced herself as Odette Treusault. I gave my name—the one known as the author of *Abandon All.*

She looked at me intently for a moment, then gave a small nod and carried on as if she didn't recognize the name. She did. Neither of the nail technicians did, or were too discreet to show it.

Quickly, I learned Odette had cruised on this ship multiple times and knew both nail technicians. She was onboard with a group she'd cruised with for decades. She and I and Imka and Odette's technician, Bennie, chatted about cruises, cruising, the schedule ahead of us, and excursions.

"We've done this so often, I've become quite the curmudgeon about excursions," Odette said. "We've done them all multiple times. Are you signed up for any?"

When Aunt Kit ran the show, we seldom joined the excursions. If she was deeply interested in a stop, she'd hire a driver and guide. Otherwise, we tramped around the town, poking into interesting corners, gathering a sense of the place along with a string of factoids, and people-watching. Always, always people-watching with Aunt Kit.

"I don't know."

As I said the words, a phrase repeated in my head. *When Aunt Kit ran the show.*

She wasn't running my show anymore. I was. I could—had to—decide for myself.

"I'll have to check them out." The excursions were a couple days off, when we stopped at a different port in the Canary Islands three days in a row.

"There's a hike into a volcano that's breathtaking." Odette chuckled. "In more ways than one. Also, if you've never ridden a camel, that is worth doing, even if it is a short ride under the tamest of circumstances. Though sometimes even then…"

Looks flickered among the other three women.

"She is onboard? Your… The, uh, other Mrs.?" Imka asked.

Clearly the other three recognized a connection between a camel ride and Imka's question. I was in the dark.

Odette asked, "Did you see her last year?" As an aside to me, she added, "I wasn't here last year. Only one couple of our group was."

"Yes," Imka said carefully. "She—"

All four of us broke off to turn toward the noise coming our way.

CHAPTER THREE

FIVE WOMEN STRODE in, like a formation of attacking jets, sharp voices rising, long hair not moving, skinny legs shrink-wrapped in capris, foot-breaker heels clacking.

Though that wasn't what I noticed first.

Let's say enhancements. On display. Almost completely on display.

"Oh, my dear, we're the amateurs," Odette murmured, apparently to herself. "They're the professionals."

Amateurs and professionals at what?

Before I could ask, the loudest voice, emanating from the one in the middle, with dark hair, a wide mouth, and hurt-your-eyes white teeth spoke without looking at anyone. "Yes, I said *now*. That should be clear enough."

"She's back, too?" Bennie muttered. "This cruise is cursed."

Imka gave her a be-quiet look.

The receptionist trailed the women, almost pleading. "But you must have appointments and—"

"We are here now. You aren't busy." This loudest woman waved toward the first open doorway. "You'll do my nails. In here."

"I have to be at the desk for other custo—"

"You won't have any customers. I'll see to that. Unless you give us the service we deserve." She swept into the room.

"And send someone to me, as well," said the next one, with hair nearly as dark, a mouth nearly as wide, and teeth nearly as white, as she strode to the next room.

"And to me." A redhead on her other side, streaked down the hall to a third room.

The receptionist scurried back to the desk, presumably to call in reinforcements.

That left one open door, past the closed door where Petronella was.

A white blonde who reminded me of a tanned praying mantis—huge eyes, skinny limbs, and a considerable butt—angled toward the door the first woman disappeared behind.

"She always thinks she comes first."

The remaining woman, slightly less blonde than the praying mantis, lips pulled back from more dazzling teeth, snarled, "You think *you* have any right to complain? You're the *new* one. I've been here longer than you."

Presumably she meant the group, not the spa, since they'd all arrived together.

"And done less. Not to mention that husband of yours who can barely afford your Botox, much less what you really need. A boob—"

The slightly less blonde of the pair piled into the blonder praying mantis with a shoulder to her diaphragm, applying a technique few females who grew up without brothers managed. It shut off the stream of words.

More, it carried both of them toward the windows.

The four of us—Odette and I in the chairs, Imka and Bennie on the stools in front of us—froze.

The hitter pulled up, digging her heels in hard enough that she stumbled to the side.

The hittee kept sailing backward toward the slanted windows.

Arms and legs spread, she splayed wide catching at supports.

She also connected with the glass. We all heard the impact. Especially where her impressive derriere landed.

Gasps echoed in a breath-held moment, wondering if the glass would hold. If it didn't, it would be a direct drop to the deck below.

The glass held.

Had to wonder if the builders' safety measures accounted for cat fights.

Imka was more practical, jumping up from her stool and grasping the woman's wrist with both hands. If the glass broke now, the woman had a chance of rescue, thanks to Imka.

"Ow. You're hurting my wrist," came the piercing whine of ingratitude.

I would have let her go, maybe—only maybe—would also have given her an extra little push into the windows. Imka held on, drawing her upright from the windows' slope and setting her on her feet, as stable as those spikes allowed. A far more impressive demonstration of strength than her earlier sweep of Petronella into the private room.

"All right, Ms. Laura?" she asked evenly.

The woman jerked free, snapping, "*Don't.*" Under her cold stare, Imka released her and stepped back.

Having driven off her savior, she rounded on her attacker.

"It's no thanks to you I'm not dead. Coral, you're a—" She bit that off with evident effort.

Coral made a sound that might indicate relief the woman she'd hit didn't go through the glass, but if so, it was mixed with residual irritation.

They glared at each other, gave simultaneous humphs of disdain, accompanied by hair tosses.

The woman who'd been spread on the windows like a praying mantis on a windshield, turned and started in one direction, leaving Coral to go the opposite way.

Odette leaned closer and said, "Window sprawler lost the skirmish, but might have won the battle."

She was right. The direction the window sprawler went was toward the remaining private room. The only way the hitter could go the opposite direction was by leaving the spa ... and the battlefield.

✧   ✧   ✧   ✧

WITH OUR NAILS looking great, Petronella and I acquainted ourselves with the ship.

At least I was acquainting myself. Petronella was listlessly lagging behind, sighing and saying she didn't know what she'd done to deserve this.

From her tone, you'd think she was being tortured by an expert. And Aunt Kit wasn't even here. I am not above torturing, especially when called upon to channel Aunt Kit's instructions. Some might even call me an expert, including some particularly whiny editors.

But from the time we'd rendezvoused at Newark airport and through our five days in Barcelona, the torturer's whip was in the other hand. Petronella was relentless in her limp, lachrymose determination to show her gratitude by "looking out" for me.

She'd asked me six thousand seven hundred and fifty-nine questions about safety measures on the ship. Honestly, I didn't know what they did if an engine blew up. Make all the drinks half price?

In her company, a dive over the railing looked more and more tempting.

She was still going on and on about safety, despite our locating the privilege lounge, the buffet, a snack bar, two other passable bars, and—most important—the soft ice cream machine.

Finding the cubbyhole saved me from going overboard before we'd left the dock.

It was perfect. A stretch of maybe fifteen outdoor deck chairs tucked in past the indoor swimming pool solarium and before stairs up to the fry-me-so-my-dermatologist-can-send-her-kids-to-college open deck above.

The indoor pool types wouldn't want to come outside. The fry-me types wouldn't like the amount of cover. Few other passengers would even know it was here.

Except two did know it was here and this gray-haired couple was ensconced in the precise middle of the line of seats. The prime spot.

He was distinguished looking. She was comfortably round.

They might be nice, but I wasn't ready to forgive them for beating me to this secret spot.

I scoped out the stairs at the far end, the door behind me to the indoor pool, the projected coverage of the overhang, and decided on the second-best (nice, but sub-prime) seat midway between the couple and the door.

"You want to stop here?" Petronella asked with a plaintive air.

Since I was already sitting, that seemed too apparent to require a reply.

"I thought you wanted to see the whole ship?"

"The rest can wait. Let's relax here."

"No, no. I'll go on and continue the tour," Petronella the Martyr said. "That way I'll know where something is if you need it."

"That's not nece—"

"I wonder where the medical center is."

"Petronella, relax. Have some fun."

"How can I when you've been so kind, so generous, so caring."

The couple looked over when we started talking. They looked away when Petronella began sniffling. I wished I could.

"There's no need—"

"There is. I want to make this trip as comfortable as possible for you. I'm going to know this ship from top to bottom."

I had a vision of the captain barring the door to the bridge against Petronella's determined weepiness. *Better him than me.*

"If that's what you want to do. I'll be here until our cabins are ready."

She sniffled, then trudged to the stairs.

I settled in with my go-bag.

The sky was blue, the sun warm without being hot, the couple murmured quietly enough to each other that I couldn't eavesdrop if I tried. Okay, I did try. Another habit learned from Aunt Kit. She maintained it was an essential tool for an author.

Or a pretend author in my case.

Eyes closed, I felt the knot between my shoulders loosen slightly. It was where I'd been storing all my repressed snap-backs at Petronella.

This was better. This was so much better.

Did the door from the pool area clanging open or did the penetrating voice of the woman assault me first? I never could sort that out.

"...and you failed to impress on that man to deliver our bags first. You know I need my—*You. What are you doing here?*"

CHAPTER FOUR

THE MOST WONDERFUL thing about cruise ships is you don't have to do a thing.

It's a reasonable and worthy use of your day to spend it stretched on a deck chair reading. To me that's the height of civilization.

The next-best wonderful thing about cruise ships is they feed you all the time and it's pretty darned good.

The awful thing about cruise ships is those two wonderful things combine into a horrible blob around the middle.

Not just mine. Nearly everyone's clothes fit tighter at the end of a cruise. It should have a name, like Murphy's Law. Maybe Gabor's Law.

Because, really, doesn't cruising make you think of the Gabor sisters? At least if you're old enough to remember them or watch *Green Acres* reruns.

The majority of transatlantic cruisers *are* old enough, one way or another to know who the Gabor sisters were.

It's one of the reasons I like Aunt Kit's choice of cruises. I'm a youngster in this crowd.

The new arrivals to my clearly not-so-secret hideaway didn't change that.

The speaker was a short woman who was more stringy than thin. Her reddish-brown hair either came out of a box or was a wig. She held a cane, though it wasn't supporting her.

Her companion was a tall, paunch-ladened man with a ring of white fluff at the back of his otherwise bald head.

His stoop-shouldered stance gave him an appearance of leaning down to the woman in what could be interpreted as a protective attitude, except for his expression of pain.

"Hello, Leah. Hello, Wardham," the man several deck chairs down from me said to the new arrivals.

I turned to look at him, but his face was as expressionless as his voice. The woman with him, though, appeared to be trying to shrink.

A sucked-in breath from the newly arrived female—Leah, presumably—turned me back to her.

"I would think that after breakfast this morning, you *two*—" Bright red lipstick reinforced the snarl her voice put in the word. "—would be ashamed to show your faces."

"We were here first," the man said evenly.

"This is *my* spot."

I'd had practically the same thought, despite never being here before. Somehow, it sounded much less reasonable when the woman named Leah snapped it aloud than it had in my head.

There was my life lesson for the day.

The clatter of the door slamming shut disrupted my absorption of the lesson sure to make me a better person. Leah moved along the deck, tapping her cane hard on the deck, and the male half of the newcomers—Wardham, the other man called him—trailed her.

Leah stopped almost at the foot of my deck chair, sparing no attention for me during her all-out glare at the couple.

That gave me the opportunity to look over the top of my reader for a closer survey.

Many people would say she was an attractive woman for her age, which I put somewhere in her seventies.

She carried herself with confidence. She had regular features, highlighted by large eyes. As small as she was, she had a strong, almost masculine-looking neck. It reminded me of a linebacker I'd dated briefly in college.

Beyond that, the impression was she'd gone too far.

Too far with the henna in her hair, which did her complexion no good, which she'd tanned too much.

Not only did the deep tan turn her arms, legs, and neck an unflattering dusty brown, but on her face, it starkly emphasized frown lines in her forehead and marionette lines from nose to mouth, then mouth to chin.

Going too red with her lipstick brought attention to those lines and spotlighted how her upper lip pulled back, in a near-snarl.

"Well?" Leah demanded. "Are you going to—?"

I half expected her to end that question with *jump overboard so I can sit where I want.*

She was interrupted by an "Oh" from the doorway, where the newest arrival stood.

This arrival I knew.

Odette Treusault paused, still holding the door. I hoped when she closed it, she'd avoid the clang.

Her gray eyes went from Leah and Wardham to the couple on the deck chairs, then to me. That last stop sparked a bit of surprise.

"Odette," said the woman on the deck chair in the middle.

Just the name. But it sounded like an SOS.

Odette didn't address it directly. Instead, she said to me, "How nice to see you again, Sheila. Have you met my friends, Maya and Ralph Russell?" She gracefully gestured to the original couple. "Maya and Ralph, this Sheila Mackey."

Remember, though, she used my writing name. She gave it a bit of extra punch the way people do when they're trying to convey more identity than the name alone might. Or when they're trying to warn someone.

Neither half of the couple on the deck chairs showed any sign of receiving the warning or recognizing the name. We exchanged hellos and quick nods, then faced Odette again.

She immediately said, "And this is Leah Treusault. And her husband, Wardham."

My brain stuttered an instant over the last name being the same as Odette's. Sisters? One married to the other's brother? Married to brothers? Or—

"Leah is married to my ex-husband, Wardham," Odette said smoothly.

Or that.

The ex and the current Mrs.

The other Mrs., Imka said. She'd meant it literally. The other Mrs. Treusault.

CHAPTER FIVE

I CONSCIOUSLY CLOSED my mouth.

Odette displayed no discomfort. She showed every indication of fulfilling a mundane social task she'd fulfilled thousands of times, always with grace.

Humor lighted her eyes as she added, "We're also bridge partners. Leah and I. Not Wardham and I." The lines at the corners of her eyes deepened. "And certainly not Wardham and Leah."

Wardham chuckled. "I'm a terrible bridge player," he confided to me.

"You wouldn't be if you paid attention," Leah said. But most of her attention was on me. Her eyes narrowed and her forehead wrinkled in the trying-to-remember-if-you're-somebody expression I'd met far frequently in the past few years than in the heady beginning of *Abandon All*'s fame.

I returned the look with an innocuous smile.

"Do I know you?" she demanded.

I stifled the smart-ass remarks about having no idea who she might know or think she knew and settled for a firm but pleasant, "No."

"You look familiar."

Odette's lips parted. I flicked a look at her. Her lips closed.

"I have that kind of face," I said cheerfully. "For some reason I always remind people of someone else. Seems to happen particularly frequently on cruises. You're not the first one. In fact, you'd bring up the rear of a very long line."

I said that with good humor and lightly.

Still, her frown deepened into a scowl.

Uh-huh. This woman did not cotton to the idea of not being original or coming in behind many others.

"Hello," I said brightly, concentrating my smile on Wardham, which he returned.

Leah gave a brief nod.

"Wardham, we'll sit down the row until my preferred spot opens."

Maya made a muffled sound. Ralph reached over and covered both her hands with one of his.

Maya seemed to shrink further as Leah pointed with her cane down the row.

"Spread my towel here, Wardham. Don't forget the clips. And you sit there." Her arrangement would have Leah looking toward Maya any time she addressed Wardham. And she wasn't done. "Take that chair, Odette."

That would put Odette on the Maya-Ralph side of Wardham. If Leah talked with Wardham or Odette, all her comments would arrow right at Maya.

Ralph, too, of course.

I zeroed in on the effect on Maya, almost forgetting Ralph, because she was more reactive.

"I'll sit here and talk with Sheila awhile." Odette gracefully dropped into the deck chair on the side closer to the door. Making me turn my back on whatever happened between those two couples.

An accident? Or deliberate?

"Have you and your friend acquainted yourself with the ship?" she asked me.

"Yes. My friend's, uh, off exploring on her own."

Under Aunt Kit's tutelage, I'd learned to carry on one conversation while eavesdropping on another. A vital skill for using people-watching to build characters, she said.

The others were also talking. Leah's voice was the only one that came through clearly enough to catch more than snatches and tone.

"…making herself ridiculous with her bleating and crying…"

Maya made a sound that I suspected Leah would call bleating.

Leah continued, "...self-centered, childish, who..."

Ralph rumbled in, so I guessed that description was directed at Maya.

Odette was saying with seeming delight, "I am familiar with this ship already. We sailed on the Diversion two and three years ago and would have last year except—" She hesitated an instant. "—something came up."

Leah said, "...after seeing what Bruce put up with year after year..."

"Do you and your, uh, friends always cruise together?"

"...think he'd have better sense, but..."

"Always." Odette's voice dropped. "Until last year—"

She broke off as a cloud covered the sun.

I turned from Odette and saw it wasn't a cloud. It was Petronella. Okay, kind of a cloud.

I was impressed and grateful she'd moved silently as a cloud and avoided clanging the door.

I introduced them. Petronella barely appeared to hear Odette's "Have you enjoyed exploring the ship?"

"I'm sorry, Sheila, they say the internet won't be turned on for at least a few more hours."

"All right." It was better than all right, but I didn't want to celebrate, I wanted her to stop talking to let me hear Leah and the others.

"I know your assistant wanted you connected to the internet right away so she could contact you."

That was a large part of why it was all right with me if the internet stayed out for the duration.

"How nice of you to look out for Sheila like this," Odette said.

"It's the least I can do." Petronella launched into another gratitude monologue.

I hated those anyhow, but particularly since as long as she talked, I missed what was going on down the row of deck chairs.

Until a chair scraping on the deck quieted Petronella and gave me an excuse to turn.

Maya shouted, "I can't take anymore."

She scrambled ungracefully out of her chair, trying to gather her belongings into the wide mouth of a bag that kept closing on her. Her visor flipped onto Ralph's knee. He calmly handed it to her, talking low enough that the words weren't decipherable, though the tone was *don't let her get to you.*

Clearly, too late. Possibly by years.

"Oh, dear," Odette murmured with a sigh. "We haven't even left port yet."

CHAPTER SIX

PETRONELLA CONTINUED LAMENTING the lack of internet as we found our way to our cabins.

Aunt Kit always said, "Best thing about these cruises. We're out of reach of assistant, agent, editor, publicist, and those other assorted people who insist on referring to themselves as 'your team.' Sounds like we run a tot's T-ball group."

Believe me, every one of these people would need the ball set up on a tee before they could hit it.

On our first cruise we brought "my" assistant. Mistake. Major mistake.

She insisted on showing me how to connect to the internet for emails from the rest of the "team." When I pretended I couldn't understand her directions, she printed out all the emails and took dictation of my replies.

She told everyone she met who I was, which meant they all talked about *Abandon All*. She gave me a running total of every calorie I put in my mouth. She suggested spa treatments to improve my on-camera appearance.

Three strikes and you're out.

No assistant came on another cruise. Supposedly because the business of—Oops. Almost let my other name slip—the brand name author now known as the human being Sheila Mackey could not possibly run without the assistant's attention every second. That's what I told the sequence of assistants who followed, anyway.

Aunt Kit might have told them the truth.

The assistants changed regularly because a couple showed hints of getting suspicious. "And they're the ones stupid enough to let their suspicions show," Aunt Kit said. "The ones to worry about are the ones who never reveal their suspicions. The ones who are too stupid not to suspect aren't good enough at the job to keep around."

After that first cruise, we took along one of Kit's relatives. Occasionally they overlapped with my relatives, but none I knew particularly well. They all thought I wrote the books. We kept to the script in their presence.

In more recent years, there'd been a couple just-graduated-from college relatives who made me feel old. They went their way, Kit went hers, and I went mine during the day. We'd meet for dinner most nights and that was plenty of family time for all of us. This laissez-faire approach even earned Kit and me "cool" points with the younger members of the family.

This time, Kit broke down and paid for Poor Petronella to go.

With me.

Kit stayed in North Carolina, saying she had far, far too much to do in settling into her new home to go on a cruise.

"Besides, you're more patient than I am."

True. Vlad the Impaler had more patience than Aunt Kit.

I was several steps closer to the Nobel Peace Prize than Vlad or Aunt Kit, but that left a whole lot of room past me on the patience continuum. In other words, don't rev up the canonization apparatus anytime soon.

Especially not after already spending several days with Poor Petronella.

"I AM ERISTO, your cabin steward, miss. Is there anything you request?"

I smiled back at the man, introduced myself with my author of *Abandon All* name and requested a bucket of ice be left in my mini-fridge daily. I prefer water on the rocks.

He brought the ice and offered to put my empty suitcase on the closet shelf, since I was at the stage of unpacking where everything was on the bed—two twins pushed together.

When I cruised with Aunt Kit, we shared a two-bedroom suite.

When she announced the arrangements for this trip, she'd told me she'd skipped the suite so I didn't have to share with Petronella.

Petronella's cabin was across the hall and maybe eight doors down—an inside room.

"I'm generous. I'm not stupid," Kit said. "Petronella will be delighted with that room, while our dignity requires at least the top line stateroom for you. If they'd have given me the discount on the suite, maybe…" She'd bought a house in the Outer Banks, but her lifetime of cost-cutting to remain solvent as an author endured when it came to more mundane matters.

So I was in a stateroom with a balcony. Not a suite. Which all suited me fine—pun intended.

Petronella and I were in our separate cabins, unpacking and settling in, after I persuaded her I didn't want her to unpack for me.

A voice came over the public address system announcing the safety drill.

The knocking on my cabin door came before the announcement finished and I didn't hear it all. On the other hand, I knew the gist from previous cruises.

"Sheila, Sheila!" Petronella shouted. "The ship is sinking! What do we do? Oh, no. Oh, no. Oh, no. We'll drown."

I snatched open the door and yanked her inside, speaking sharply to break through her panic.

"It's *not* sinking. It's not even moving yet. This is a drill. Teaches you what to do if there *is* an emergency. If you're not quiet, listen to every word, and remember every word, and there is an emergency— like the ship sinking—you will drown."

That stopped her from talking, though I feared she'd hyperventilate.

She clung to my arm and made occasional whimpering sounds as we made our way to the assigned spot.

Not hard to find with crew members in fluorescent vests and big signs indicating which way passengers assigned to each group should go.

The crew member in charge of our muster group was a young man with skin tanned nearly as dark as his hair and eyes.

Unsmiling, he directed us into place within lines marked on the deck, recommending taller people move toward the back, to increase the number of people who'd be able to see him.

"*I'm* not moving to the back." Leah's easily recognizable voice topped all other talkers and ambient noise. "I don't care what some idiot says. He'd get us all drowned."

The crew member's face darkened.

The people in front of me shifted uneasily, and I saw Leah … standing in the next group.

How strange.

I mean it was strange for anyone to be nasty at muster drill, plus his instructions didn't apply to her, since she was short, and he wasn't even her muster leader.

Before she could say more, the captain's voice came over the PA system, drawing everyone's attention. Or almost everyone's.

I could still see Leah's lips moving. Wardham bent as if to listen to her.

Our muster leader moved as far from Leah as he could while still having anything to do with our area.

He didn't budge as he gave us the instructions. I hoped people on the far side had good hearing or they'd get no benefit from this.

✧   ✧   ✧   ✧

PETRONELLA HAD LISTENED for two—her and me.

She proved it by repeating the instructions on a loop as we returned to our cabins.

With the elevators jammed, a lot of people streamed down or up the stairways. Each set of stairs climbed halfway to the next deck, then turned 180 degrees and made the rest of the trip. We followed a stream going up. Ahead of us, I saw Ralph and Maya. Three steps higher, putting them a full half-flight higher than us, were Leah and Wardham.

I looked around but didn't see Odette. Had Ralph and Maya been with Leah and Wardham and I hadn't noticed, while focused on Leah's behavior? Possible.

Leah, gripping the handrail and using her cane with the other hand, stopped abruptly on the second-half stretch of stairs to deck seven. She stared up, presumably to where others were climbing to the halfway landing to deck eight. She muttered something but I didn't catch it.

Swearing, from her expression.

Certainly, the people stopped behind her were inclined toward grumbles.

The stoppage rippled to where I stood. A man behind me asked—not in a holiday mood—"What's the holdup?"

As if seeking the answer, I leaned over the railing and twisted to look up, well past where I knew the holdup originated with Leah. Instead, I tried to see what caught her attention.

Mostly I saw feet through the open space where risers would otherwise be. Male feet, female feet. Tennis shoes, flat sandals, tottering-high-heeled sandals, flip-flops, orthopedic shoes.

I couldn't identify what Leah was looking at.

She half raised her cane, as if she might hit anyone in front of her. But no one was there, because they'd moved on, while she'd stalled.

"C'mon, lady," the man behind me called.

Leah started with a wide-angle glare, then focused on me, as if I'd suddenly become a baritone.

I smiled broadly at her.

It was a trick Aunt Kit had told me before the *Abandon All* interviews started. Someone tries to intimidate you, hit them with a big old smile. Throws them off their stride and makes them wonder what they missed.

Leah started up the stairs, still looking at me.

The smile started to hurt.

CHAPTER SEVEN

WE WERE ASSIGNED to the later dinner seating.

Not by the cruise line. By Aunt Kit.

It was the time she preferred and perhaps she thought I preferred it, too, though she never asked. As a matter of fact, I did prefer it. I also was used to it.

Or, suggested a dark, suspicious corner of my mind, Aunt Kit selected it because she knew Petronella would hate it.

"Oh, no, I couldn't possibly. It's so late," she'd moaned at least once every half hour since five o'clock.

"It's the same time we ate in Barcelona. But if you're hungry, you don't have to wait for our time in the dining room, you can eat at the buffet."

"Oh, I'm not *hungry*. It's just so *late*."

By the time we were waiting in line outside the dining room—she'd knocked on my door twenty minutes early, sure it would take forever to reach the dining room and if we weren't there on the dot they would lock us out—I tried another tack.

"You know, Petronella, back at home it's not late at all. It's not even two-thirty in the afternoon."

"Two-thirty? That's so early for dinner."

The maître d' began welcoming diners at the moment. Saving me. Possibly saving Petronella.

We were directed to a great table.

No outside view, but that didn't matter since it was dark. Not within sight or sound of the kitchen doors, but close enough to avoid what Aunt Kit called the *English Manor Issue* of food being cold by the time it reached you. Our table for two sat ten inches from a matching one, which gave the option to mingle or not with the people at the next table. On previous cruises, Kit tended not to mingle, I usually did.

Another benefit of our table was I had a great view of most of the dining room, with only the corner behind me cut off.

The couple at the table next to us arrived and introduced themselves as Catherine and Bob. They were Scottish, with dry and roguish senses of humor, experienced cruisers, and good story-tellers.

They talked past the "oh-no-I-couldn'ts" and persuaded Petronella to order two appetizers as we conspired to cover all the menu's offerings and share tastes. I should say Bob persuaded her. Her unsubtle reliance on his opinion made me squirm, until Catherine, sitting next to me, caught my eye and winked.

They were older than Petronella, yet treated her with a soothing courtesy that relaxed her. I was grateful. And reminded myself that impatience—one of my fortes—only agitated her more.

Waiting for the appetizers, I glanced around.

The faux marble pillars, pastoral mural, and multiple reflective surfaces weren't my taste, but the room, carved into smaller groupings by curved banquettes, was people-watching paradise.

I won't detail all the interesting groups and pairings—though a couple not far away were fascinating for how totally unexpressive and untalkative they were—but limit myself to tables that included people I'd already met.

A table for eight, angled slightly left of straight ahead, included Odette, Leah, and Maya, as well as Wardham and Ralph. Three bottles of wine stood on the table, already well depleted.

One seat was empty with the other two assigned to an attractively average couple, perhaps in their early fifties. I'd bet they would beg the maître d' to change their seats by the next meal.

And not because of Maya or Ralph or Wardham and certainly not because of charming Odette.

Leah Treusault.

The empty chair separated her from the woman in the spare couple. Insufficient barrier, as I knew from the deck chairs earlier. Plus, the angle gave her a direct shot at the male half of the spare couple. Odette, across from the empty chair, seemed to try to deflect Leah's impact on the younger couple, both by interacting with them and by redirecting Leah's attention toward Wardham.

Leah barely glanced at him before turning back to the younger couple.

Fresh blood.

The phrase came into my head in Aunt Kit's voice. But I suspected it was my brain that saw Leah as a carnivorous predator.

She was more commanding than loud, though she was loud enough that her conversations could never qualify as entirely private.

Leah's interest in another table prompted me to turn my head farther to the left and see the five Valkyries—or should it be Harpies—from the spa, each with a corresponding male, at a round table for ten in the center.

You'd think it would be easy to pair them up into couples. Heck it was fifty-fifty, since they alternated male and female around the table. But I couldn't spot any favoritism in the touching and talking and flirting.

None at that table paid attention to anyone or anything beyond their group. From my angle it was impossible to tell for sure if one individual was the object of Leah's attention or if it was the entire table.

I switched back to the table for ten. Nope. Still couldn't track the precise direction of her interest.

I did notice, however, they'd already killed seven bottles of wine, as well as having a mixed drink at each place.

Her gaze following the direction of mine, Catherine asked, too quietly for our companions to hear, "Father-daughter night?" Then she answered her own question. "Dear me, no, for if they were fathers they'd surely tell those daughters to dress more appropriately."

I smiled my agreement.

She subtly looked toward the table again, then returned her gaze to me. "I recall a number of them from other cruises."

"Do you?"

"Oh, yes. Any number of people make the trip regularly. Bob and I aren't in the every year club, but we come now and then."

The appetizers arrived, naturally monopolizing the conversation at the same time it broadened to include Petronella and Bob.

Dinner was delightful. For the company as well as the food. As much as I liked Bob and Catherine, I might have liked their effect on Petronella even more. I could feel my shoulders releasing and my forehead smoothing.

We were lingering over multiple desserts—once again shared amongst us—when a new voice rose high and loud.

"Oh! Oh! You're that writer. The one who wrote *Abandon All* when you were a baby." The part about writing *Abandon* when I was a baby did not compensate for this tall woman with the strong French accent outing me the first night. Some had already left the dining room, but the remaining heads turned toward this beacon of noise.

"How kind of you. Won't you sit down?" I pushed at the empty chair behind me to encourage her. That would lessen the attention. It also would stop her from half climbing over Catherine's back.

Besides, I had this routine down. Give a few responses to her effusions about *Abandon All*, then switch the conversation. Aunt Kit sometimes grumbled that I shut off the spigot of praise too soon because I hadn't slaved over the book the way she had.

True.

But she hadn't listened to people talking about it as much as I had.

To end the encounter for good, I brought out the big guns, by questioning the fan about "my" other books.

Some made a graceful exit. Others, like this woman, scrambled hard for the lifeboat to escape the sinking ship of their interest in the conversation.

Okay, again, not the best metaphor. I had to stop thinking about ships sinking.

CHAPTER EIGHT

MUSIC DREW ME toward the Wayfarer Bar after Petronella and I left Catherine and Bob outside the dining room.

They were heading toward a show and invited us to join them. I'd declined. Petronella said *Oh, no, I couldn't*, without indicating why she couldn't.

Unlike too many musical performances I'd heard on cruises, what came from the Wayfarer Bar was actually, well, musical.

"I'm going to stop in here for a nightcap. Want to come?" I asked Petronella.

"If you don't mind and you think you'll be…"

"I'll be just fine." To support her faltering step toward expressing her desire, I added, "This is your vacation, too. Do what you want. What *do* you want to do?"

"I'd like to go to my cabin and have an early night." Before I could endorse that option, Petronella became flustered. "I should say to *your* cabin. Not where you're staying, but your cabin nonetheless, since you so generously paid for it."

I thought she'd run the excessive gratitude tank empty. Apparently she'd rested enough to refill it.

"Kit did all the work." As well as paying, but that had to remain our secret. "She planned the whole thing." At this moment I wasn't as grateful as I probably should have been. "About all I did was meet you at the airport and follow Kit's instructions."

"No, no, no. I know how very much I owe you for your kindness. I'm sure Kit did some, helped you in little ways as she has while she's lived with you and as I'm determined to do in her absence. But I know who is truly behind this great kindness in my time of need and I can't possibly thank you en—"

"Kit. All Kit. Like the manicure. All she left for me to do was hand you that unlimited ShipCard and say *Knock yourself out.*"

"Oh, no. I couldn't possibly… To impose on you by using that card. No, no, no."

"It's already paid for, Petronella. If you don't use it, it goes to waste."

"But surely you could get a refund."

I shook my head firmly. I had no idea how the things worked, but I wasn't letting any uncertainty show. "No refunds. Only thing to do at this point is get the most value from it by using it all the time."

"Then perhaps I should…" She cast a weary look toward the entrance of the bar.

"The only *should* is to do what you want." I turned her, then took her shoulders from behind. "Rest up tonight. If you feel like being a party animal, we'll dance the night away tomorrow."

I nudged her shoulders to start her away from me. She continued moving that direction, but looked back with a sad, slightly scolding smile. "Oh, no, no, I couldn't possibly."

I COULD FIND a seat, then wait for a server to come take my drink order.

But as I walked in, I saw only one server attending several groups beyond where a man with a guitar and woman with a violin sat and played the music that had drawn me.

Another look showed one of those groups was Odette, Leah, and the others. They had empty glasses in front of them and Ralph tried to catch the server's attention.

Another server showed for an instant, then was recalled to the area reserved for those in the cruise line's loyalty program. I caught a glimpse of the spa quintet's leader and the window-sprawler there.

If they duplicated their table's rate of alcoholic consumption at dinner, they'd have that server tied up for good.

I diverted to the bar.

The redhead from the spa invaders sat on a stool, elbows on the countertop, leaning forward. Which had to give the bartender a mighty fine view down the front of her dress.

The guy next to her—not either of the men she'd sat between at dinner, so presumably not her husband—tried for the same view, but he had a difficult angle to gawk effectively.

She said something, looking at the bartender through her lashes.

He laughed. Loudly. Echoed by the guy next to her.

The guitar player's head jerked toward the sound. He glared. The woman next to him, with her hands and head occupied with the violin, nudged him with her knee.

He looked at her. Her raised eyebrows acknowledged his right to be irked, but reminded him it did no good. Or maybe I was reading a lot into raised eyebrows.

Apparently, he did, too.

He angled away from the bar.

Through all this—accomplished in a flash—the music never faltered. They were good. Really good. With something deeper than what sounded to me like impressive technical skill. They were connected.

They truly made music together.

The bartender had caught the musician's reaction, but he was more focused on the redhead departing. "No need to—"

"Thanks for the restaurant tip," she said loudly and casually.

She pushed past me, her motion turning me partially away from the bar or risk being knocked over. I saw her slide her arm around the neck of a shorter man I'd seen her with in the dining room and now guessed was her husband. She leaned into him as they walked past the musicians and toward the area in back reserved for the frequent cruisers.

"*Musicians.* Damned touchy *artistes.* We're all supposed to sit here like we're in church and I get nothing in tips. That's not right," the bartender grumbled.

Was his grumble about tips? Or being deprived of sight-seeing the redhead?

I'd tip him—but not offer sights—if I could get past the guy who'd been sitting next to the redhead, but his splayed out legs blocked me. And then another man slid onto the stool the redhead abandoned and gave his order.

Sheesh.

The bartender came out of his funk over the loss of the redhead to begin pouring drinks.

The guy blocking me shoulder-butted the newcomer, who drew back in surprise or displeasure or both.

"See that bottle, second from the left," the first guy said, with no sign he'd noticed the other man's withdrawal. "That sailboat on the label? That was my grandfather's boat. I used to have a little boat at the same yacht club. Before the place got overrun. You know. Not our sort."

Now the newcomer looked offended.

The guy in front of me gave no sign of noticing as he went on about sailboats—his, his grandfather's, and other people's—and how they could not possibly stay in some marina where they'd be rubbing hulls with sailboats belonging to lesser mortals.

The bartender delivered his drink then and he turned, showing off one of those tans that makes you think of dust bowls.

Bad enough he blocked me from placing my order, letting the man who'd arrived after me get in first, but now he looked me up and down like he was doing me a favor.

"Excuse me—" My tone meant he should be excusing himself. "—I want to order."

"I bet you do." He tried to make it suggestive, which made no sense.

"Excuse me." That dripped ice.

The guy who'd slipped in ahead of me must have ordered something simple, because he turned away already. I sidestepped Mr. Grandpa's Sailboat on the Label to get that bar-front spot. As I did, Mr. Sailboat brushed his palm against my hip and started around to my derriere.

I jerked away to leave a gap between us. "Do not touch me." Not loud, but distinct enough to turn a few nearby heads, including the bartender's.

"Jason," I said to the bartender, cribbing off the nametag, "you will need to call security immediately if this passenger bothers me any further."

"Yes, ma'am. Do you want me to, uh…"

I held Mr. Grandpa's Sailboat on the Label's gaze. He'd gone red of cheek and neck, but assumed a smirky grin and raised his hands in would-be innocence, barely missing dribbling his scotch on me. "I'm leaving. No need for hysterics."

Forget security, I'd throttle the guy myself. Hysterics, my—

I bit my tongue, held my cool, and Mr. Grandpa's Sailboat on the Label went away.

"I'm sorry, ma'am. If you'd like me to call—"

"What I'd like is a glass of champagne."

Perhaps by way of amends, Jason came through with Veuve Clicquot.

Jason was in my good books, as my tip showed him.

✧   ✧   ✧   ✧

I TOOK A chair by a window. A couple sitting across from me smiled briefly, then returned to absorption in the music. Perfect.

I know a lot of passengers enjoy the energy of the shows in the theaters. I'm closer to Aunt Kit's viewpoint.

She maintains the shows are impossible to listen to because they are too loud. "How can anyone say they're any good when the volume is cranked so high it distorts the music? After a few I doubt that's an accident."

Had I learned that attitude from her?

But these musicians were good. The guitar and violin supported and enhanced each other. Sometimes swapping the expected roles of strength (guitar) and sweetness (violin), making the most familiar song fresh.

It was lovely.

Except for bursts of sound from the frequent cruisers room.

One particularly raucous episode of laughter, hoots, and shouts prompted me to turn my head.

I couldn't see the offenders, but I saw Leah standing and starting toward the back area. Odette caught her arm, slowing her, but she would have kept going if Ralph Russell hadn't stood in her way.

Although I couldn't hear her, I could see Leah saying things to him. Not nice things.

He stood without responding. She gradually ran out of steam.

Odette said something, possibly about the musicians, judging by her gesture toward them.

Leah finally sat, turning toward the music.

When the musicians took a break, I opted to leave.

Odette's group remained. As did the loud group in back. I raised a hand in acknowledgement of Jason's Veuve Clicquot largesse, but didn't stop to say good-night. I would cement his Veuve Clicquot pours another time. Mr. Grandpa's Sailboat on the Label had returned.

I left humming the last song played, knowing the tune was familiar but unable to capture its name.

CHAPTER NINE

THE THING ABOUT cruising is that, while eavesdropping is hard to avoid—at least for some of us—you can, in general, have as much or as little discourse as you like with your fellow passengers.

There are those who know the name of the majority of their fellow travelers—passengers and crew—by the end of the voyage. There are others who smile amiably, pass the odd comment on the weather or the likely flavor of the red dessert second from the left, but otherwise go their own way.

There are a few who make their presence known and felt.

Yes, Leah Treusault came to mind. Petronella, too, though for different reasons.

Even at poolside the next day, even while I read, she discoursed me relentlessly, relating in great detail how she'd watched two passengers take towels without checking them out according to the rules.

I felt sorry for anyone eavesdropping. I felt sorry for me.

When she discovered she'd left her sunscreen in her cabin, I did not offer to share the tube in my bag.

I read in blissful peace for several chapters.

Only when I heard "Oh dear, oh dear, oh dear, excuse me, sorry, excuse me, oh dear, oh dear, oh dear" heralding Petronella's return did I realize she'd been gone a considerable time.

She collapsed into her deck chair beside me.

Her hands were empty. None of the pockets in the long-sleeved smock she wore over knit pants bulged.

"Where's your sunscreen?"

"Oh! I forgot. I never reached my cabin, I was that upset. A passenger fell on the stairs. I was right there. I was going down. She and her friend were going up. Poor thing. Horrible, horrible, horrible. She screamed in pain. Well, after she regained consciousness she did. Then she—"

"She was knocked out?"

"—screamed. Though, first, she sort of whimpered and made moaning sounds. Oh, yes. She was unconsciousness. She fell backward and hit her head on the landing. And she must have been up at least three steps. I didn't see her until she started to fall. She sort of squawked. She screamed later, after she came to," she explained earnestly, as if I might have thought she screamed while unconscious. "It must have hurt her poor head. That's why I took off my sweater and put it under her head, to cushion it from the hard floor."

"She asked you to—?"

"The poor thing wasn't conscious yet. But it was only common decency. Though *some* would have denied her comfort," she said with dark disapproval. "The emotion of that poor girl falling…"

I was torn. My curiosity nudged me to try to find out more. My experience of Petronella said I wouldn't get much information, though there'd be lots of words.

"Everyone crowded around, saying things, but I acted. For her comfort. Poor soul. Her friend standing there, doing absolutely nothing. Even when she screamed, it was clear she was in shock."

I needn't have wrestled with whether to ask her questions. Her words flowed on.

"She insisted it wasn't her silly high heels, though of course it was. She kept saying she'd tripped. On those shoes, as anybody could see. I was telling her that when the medical team arrived and said what she needed was peace and quiet. They sent everyone away. I had to stay, though, because I was a witness and there was a ship's officer asking questions. And they still had my sweater."

"You don't have it now, either," I pointed out. The thought of adding that sweater to what she already wore made me realize I'd become quite warm myself, sitting in this sun.

"No, no, I don't. They were so kind, so considerate. They begged me to get on with my day and enjoy it and they promised to have my sweater delivered to the cabin when they moved the young woman."

"Good, good. I'm going in the pool." I stashed my reading device and started to unbutton my coverup. "How about you?"

"Oh, no, I couldn't possibly," was her unsurprising response.

Turned out, as she informed me, she refused to own, much less wear, a swimsuit.

"Oh, no, I couldn't possibly," she repeated. But in this instance her tone implied she'd made a moral choice and those who didn't make the same choice were somehow immoral. Or, at the very least, demonstrating seriously flawed judgment.

I'm about in the normal range of figures. I have friends and family, though, who allow themselves to be limited by their own or others' tut-tutting—real or imagined—into never venturing into a pool on a hot day. One of the most satisfying sensations there is.

In this moment, Petronella represented all that held back my mother, my great-aunt, my dear friends from enjoying that sensation.

It griped me, despite my best resolutions not to be griped by her or at her.

"Well, I can." I stood and dropped my coverup, refusing to feel self-conscious. I also took out the sunscreen and handed it to her. "Even if you stay here, you need this. But you should come in the pool, too."

"Oh, no, I couldn't possibly." Though she did take the sunscreen.

I walked toward the pool.

"Sheila!" Petronella cried.

I turned back.

"Are you sure? Is it safe? I mean…" She dropped her voice to a stage whisper. "Can you swim?"

I made brief eye contact with the young man "life-guarding" for a pool that was to Olympic pools what T-ball was to the major leagues.

He didn't quite wink.

I limited myself to a firm and cheerful, "Yes."

As I spent a good amount of time floating in the outdoor pool, with timeouts in a hot tub, I found myself applauding all—but especially the women—who braved swimsuits regardless of whether their shape matched the prevailing views of body beautiful.

✧ ✧ ✧ ✧

FROM THE MACHINE that dispenses soft ice cream into cones, where I'd stopped for a mid-afternoon snack, I recognized the voice of Grandpa's Sailboat on the Label rising over recorded reggae music.

"Don't be chintzy on the scotch."

Past the ice cream machine, I could look down the line of stools at the poolside bar, which had some exotic name, but everybody called the poolside bar. The bartender—younger than Jason, with golden skin, whether from sun or genes—flushed, turned away from the customer and lifted the bottle. But he didn't put more alcohol in the glass, which looked to my unpracticed eye to be at regulation level.

The Grandpa's Sailboat on the Label guy sat sideways, his back mostly to me. His position gave him a clear view of the closest hot tub.

I was glad I'd used only the farthest hot tub.

The young bartender added ice and turned back to the man. "Here you are, sir."

Would he fall for it?

I took a healthy lick of my ice cream cone.

"That's better. Used to be you could get a decent drink on these bathtubs, but—" He broke off to drink.

"What did you say before about the woman who fell on the stairs?"

I suspected encouraging passengers to gossip didn't get a lot of space in the crew member's manual, but I approved his ploy to redirect this annoying grandson of the boat owner on the bottle.

I settled in to a good licking rhythm and listened.

"She went down like a sack of bricks. *Bam.* Going up the stairs one second, falling backward the next, and *wham* on her head. She'd've had padding if she'd landed on her ass." Time out for him to laugh at his own witticism. "Though her friend would have had even more. The *badunkadonk* on that one ... Anyway, some idiot woman, who'd first screamed like a banshee, kept trying to pull her around and stuff something under her head. I kept saying 'Don't move her. Don't move her at all.' "

Petronella? Had to be. I sure hoped the woman who fell wasn't litigious. Though she couldn't get anything from Petronella, since she had nothing.

"In the meantime, the other knockoff Housewives of Wherever low-rent trophy wives come from—" He hadn't been critical when he'd been ogling the redhead or now, describing their derrieres. "—who was with her stood like a statue with no expression at all. She might as well have been doing her nails for all the attention she paid to her friend."

The bartender said something too low for me to catch.

"Yeah, yeah, you're right. Barracudas, for sure. Who—"

"I didn't say—" the young bartender started in alarm.

"—needs friends like that, huh? But at least she wasn't doing the woman on the ground harm like that screamer. I told her—first rule, don't move the person. But she kept yanking the woman's head and stuffing things under it. Finally, a crew member showed up and got rid of everybody.

"I was glad to go. Let the professionals help her and it got me away from the iceberg would-be-friend and the hysterical old bat."

He gestured widely with his glass, flinging ice cubes and dribbles of liquid. The bartender jumped back. Not fast enough.

"Gotta move quicker, kid. But you got that supply of clean stuff over by the buffet." He started to turn on the bar stool toward me.

I stepped back where the wall would block his view of me, then around another corner, as the young bartender appeared from the opposite side of an elevator bank, heading toward the buffet area. I took the final bite of ice cream, disposed of the last inch of cone, then caught the elevator.

CHAPTER TEN

PETRONELLA CONFIDED TO Bob and Catherine at dinner that she feared I'd gotten too much sun that day.

I'd seen a faint pink when I changed for dinner and that was only compared to the stark white of the towel folded into a bunny that Eristo had left on the bed.

"She looks fine to me," Bob said heartily. "Healthy and better rested than she did last night. Few more weeks of that treatment and she'll be beyond blooming."

"Thank you, Bob." I hadn't been aware of not feeling rested, but now that he mentioned it...

Petronella immediately accepted his view as gospel and didn't bring it up again. That definitely contributed to my rested feeling.

After we'd ordered and the waitstaff left us, Catherine leaned in close.

"Did you hear? The passenger who fell on the stairs today—you knew of that?—is hurt worse than they feared. They're concerned about her neck."

I closed my eyes an instant. Petronella had lifted the woman's head to jam a sweater under it. *Please, let the woman be okay. And please don't let Petronella be the cause if she isn't.*

"That poor soul." Petronella, with no apparent linking in her mind between her sweater-jamming and potential neck problems, told Catherine and Bob about being there when the woman fell. They exclaimed over her.

My relief that she hadn't mentioned her sweater activities deepened when Catherine said in a low voice, "I heard they're worried about paralysis."

Petronella covered her mouth too late to stop a gasp that turned a few heads. "How horrible."

Catherine sat back, looking innocuous.

"Any idea who she is?" I asked quietly.

Bob gave a scoffing, *huh*. "Of course, she does."

With a casualness to inform anyone watching that she wasn't saying anything the least bit interesting, she said, "Have you encountered a group of, ah, younger wives of older men? I see you have. This is—"

"She's blonde," Petronella interrupted.

I looked from her to Catherine. "Really, really light blonde?"

"Blonde," Petronella said.

"Not as light as another in their group," Catherine said. "Piper has the lightest blonde hair. Coral is the one who fell."

Interesting. That made Piper the one who'd gone into the windows. But Imka had called her Ms. Laura. Last name, presumably. I wondered where Piper Laura had been when her opponent in that great spa duel went down the stairs.

Wait a minute. Mr. Grandfather's Sailboat on the Label had said the friend of the faller had quite the *badunkadonk*—"

That sounded like Piper.

"Coral fell? Not Piper?"

Catherine tipped her head. "That surprises you?"

It did.

Why? They were walking up the stairs together, didn't that indicate they'd reached equilibrium, if not an accord?

Catherine's voice pulled me back. "Why are you smiling, Bob?"

"I heard something, too. We're swinging in close to land to drop her off in Gibraltar. Should be pretty seeing the lights at night up close."

"Oh, but that poor woman, to miss the rest of cruise," Petronella protested.

"Doesn't hurt her anymore if we enjoy the lights. Might as well."

Catherine patted his hand. "My practical Robert. Can you pity me for living with such an entire lack of sentiment?"

Petronella looked uncomfortable at the joking lament.

Bob looked thoroughly satisfied with his wife's touch and words.

I grinned.

Catherine didn't quite quell the twitch of her lips.

✧ ✧ ✧ ✧

AFTER DINNER, CATHERINE lured Petronella away from her perceived duties as my watchdog by saying she needed a bingo partner, since Bob's failure to pay close attention to the calls had surely cost her thousands in winnings over the years.

Catherine winked at me over her shoulder as they departed.

With gratitude in my heart, I went to the Wayfarer Bar for a quiet drink alone.

Jason was not behind the bar tonight, so no Veuve Clicquot.

Nor were the musicians here. So no hope of identifying the song that had become an earworm.

Instead, there was a young man with a strong accent, trying to run a trivia game. The most frequent question back at him from the players—including me—was "What?"

No one, from any country, appeared to be able to comprehend his accent. He finally resorted to pantomime when none of us could unravel Al-pa-hand as elephant.

In the end, it wasn't that anyone won the trivia game as much as the last person still trying got the grand prize—a cruise line pen. I'd quit two rounds earlier. Darn.

With that distraction over, I sipped at my drink and realized a couple had come in while I tried to unravel the trivia questions/pantomime and now sat directly across a small table from me.

The intricacies and intimacies of the woman's family history unfolded in detail, as if a person feet away—say, me—couldn't hear them.

I tried to block it out, but I'm no good at that. I might never have been good at it. After the years with Aunt Kit, I'd become an always-on radar dish pulling in signals.

Kit maintained eavesdropping was a vital tool for creating characters and their stories.

Quickly, I learned that the woman had a cousin who got married late in life, followed his wife to a "settlement, no more, well east of Calgary, in the middle of the plains" and was now raising two small children. Because the wife up and left him and the "settlement."

"I think she's realized now how much of a—" She said a word that made me blink. "—he was."

He was? He was the one stuck in isolation *she'd* picked, then left. And he was raising the kids, while she took off.

"She's thinking about what's good for her at last. She's shaken off his spell," the man said.

Good for her? What about those kids?

This was the drawback to eavesdropping that Aunt Kit never seemed to experience. She absorbed what people said, who they were and stored it away to use for a character at some future time without getting involved with the real people. Her characters, yes. But not the people who'd contributed real life stuff to their creation.

Me? I wanted to argue with them. I wanted to set them straight. I wanted them to give the cousin who was, "late in life," raising two kids, alone, out on the plains, a break. Heck, I wanted to go find the guy and give him a hug.

Aunt Kit would warn me he might be a pervert.

"Sheila. Did you hear?" Catherine was beside me, ending my force-fed eavesdropping and my cogitations about Aunt Kit.

"Hear what?"

"Bob was right. We're swinging close to Gibraltar, much closer than planned. They're not only dropping off that young woman who fell on the stairs, they're taking her to the hospital there. They feel she needs more specialized care than the ship's medical staff can give her."

"Paralysis? She's that much worse than they thought?"

"Not necessarily—"

The PA system came to life with a mechanical clearing of its throat. "This is your captain," the voice said, before pretty much repeating what Catherine said. Though not as succinctly.

"How did you know that?" I asked when the captain signed off. "Good grief, you could have written that announcement. Or at least read it beforehand."

She gave an airy, dismissive wave. "You learn a thing or two when you've cruised as much as I have."

"You said *not necessarily* when I said she must be hurt badly. What did you mean?"

"Oh, that. Word is that she was quite the thorn in their bums and the medical staff can't wait to get her off." She took my elbow and tugged me up. "C'mon. Bob and Petronella went up top to save us spots at the rail. Let's go see Gibraltar."

CHAPTER ELEVEN

THE SHIP SLOWED. Slowed more.

The backseat captains gathered at the railing on the top deck, speculated how and where the ship would approach the port of Gibraltar.

A string of city lights along the shore reflected into the water, doubling its impact. At first narrow, the string unfurled, growing brighter and thicker, like diamonds in a necklace design that became bolder yet could not compete with the huge, glittering rock at the end.

The lit face of the Rock of Gibraltar rose in sheer, illuminated mass.

"*That* is impressive," I murmured.

I'd passed it before in cruising with Aunt Kit, but never this close.

From those other trips, I knew the rock was the eastern end of the strait. And it wasn't the closest Spain and Africa came to meeting, that came a little farther west-southwest along the Spanish coast. But that huge rock was the emotional demarcation of leaving behind the Mediterranean Sea and embarking into the Atlantic Ocean.

No wonder the ancients considered it one of the twin pillars of Hercules and the end of the known world.

A perfect image for my life. This trip was the end of my known world and I was about to embark on a voyage into unknown territory, with great possibilities, but also great dang—

"Are you famous?"

Pop. There went the balloon of my exalted mood of fear and exhilaration.

"No." Firm, but polite. I mastered that tone years ago.

"Somebody said you're famous." I realized the voice came from the woman who had led the five into the spa. Queen of the Harpies. Something more firm and less polite might be needed to shake off this woman. "What do you do?"

The heck if I know.

But I was still the public face of Aunt Kit's literary creation for a few more days. "I'm an author."

"Oh."

I bit my lip to not laugh. Those two letters not only conveyed her complete lack of interest in books or those who wrote them, but also irritation she'd been hoodwinked by someone into thinking I was worthy of interest.

She started to turn away, but the redhead came in closer with an odd look on her face.

"You had some book that was made into a movie, didn't you?" she demanded.

"Yes."

"A big movie."

"In some quarters."

"You *are* famous," accused the first one.

"I can't be famous or you'd know me."

After a couple breaths, the dark-haired leader's face cleared. She found my logic persuasive, but the redhead with the odd look wasn't satisfied. To forestall her, I said to them, "It's your friend who's being taken to the hospital, isn't it? I'm surprised you're not seeing her off."

"Her husband's with her," the leader said with little interest.

"What a shame that happened, especially at the start of the cruise. Is she okay?"

"Yeah. She'll be fine." The redhead oozed empathy ... but only in an upside-down universe. "What movie?"

Why was I answering this inquisition? Oh, yeah. Aunt Kit.

"*Abandon All.*"

The redhead's eyes changed to boredom. I realized what had been odd before—she'd been frowning with only her eyes because her facial muscles didn't move.

"I never seen—I don't recall that movie," the leader said.

"Artsy-fartsy," the redhead said.

Mildly, I said, "A classic."

The redhead sniffed. But the leader didn't write me off entirely. Because she said, "See you 'round," before she swept off in her skyscraper shoes.

Heels can elongate and highlight the wearer's legs. But her calves bunched into obtrusive knots under her tight leggings.

The redhead gave me an unfriendly final look before following.

A BOAT THAT had come up to the Diversion, presumably for Coral, took off toward a point someone declared was the hospital, his expertise coming from Google maps.

While most of the observers left during the Diversion's maneuvers away from Gibraltar, I stayed up late with a few other railbirds to watch us complete the passage through the strait and exchange the Mediterranean Sea for the Atlantic Ocean.

One of those railbirds said he'd served as chaplain for British forces in Gibraltar and entertained us with tales, some possibly tall tales. Enjoyable, nonetheless.

I woke the next morning to dreams of mice in the walls, which was one of Aunt Kit's constant worries about the brownstone having encountered the problem in several places she'd lived before making a living wage writing. One of her interview questions for household help was how they felt about killing mice. If they started talking about the Disney version of Cinderella and how the mice became white horses to carry her to the ball, they were out.

It took a few moments to realize where I was and that the scratching was at the cabin door.

I opened it to Petronella. "Oh, good. You're awake." She breezed inside. I followed, half comatose. "You'll never guess."

After a minute or two of silence I realized she wanted me to accidentally guess at something she'd said I'd never guess. I settled for

"What?"

"They returned my sweater."

Sweater? Returned? ... The one she'd wrenched that Coral woman's head up to stuff in. Florence Nightingale she wasn't. "Good."

"Not only that, she had it cleaned for me. Wasn't that nice?"

"Uh-huh." I'd bet it was the crew, not Coral who'd seen to that detail.

"But you're not dressed," Petronella observed.

What do you say to something like that? I grunted.

"Don't you want breakfast?"

"It's being served for another hour and a half." A possibility began to form in my sleep-shrouded brain. "I might skip breakfast today. But you should go down and get some."

"Without you?"

"Absolutely. You can't let me deprive you of sustenance." I saw the argument brewing in her head. "I'd feel awful. You don't want me to feel awful, do you?"

I'd cornered her with her own determination to coddle me into oblivion.

"But..."

I guided her toward the door and sent her on her way. Then I went back to sleep.

✧   ✧   ✧   ✧

ON MY WAY to stake out a nice sunny deck chair by the pool, the buffet supplied me with breakfast. Next stop was to get a couple towels. I joined the line to hand over my ShipCard so I could be charged if I failed to return the towels.

"Watch this."

It wasn't a kid asking for a parent's attention.

It was a command from an empress to a serf.

It was Leah's voice over my shoulder with that order.

I'd been whiling away the wait wondering if this practice of monitoring towel usage arose because passengers absconded with towels in their luggage (Why? They felt like cardboard), because towels were flung overboard in great quantities in exuberant good spirits (How? They'd make lousy kites), or because they were left all over the ship and someone had to pick them up (Were they any harder to pick up than empty glasses and dirty dishes?).

Despite myself, Petronella's tale of the towel-grabbers from yesterday resurfaced. It would be easy to grab a towel from the far side of the large rack of clean ones, which would block the view of the crew members giving them out. On various cruises I'd see any number of passengers snag a towel without a crew member seeing or, at least, not letting on that they'd seen.

That left us rule-followers to creep forward toward the counter where our accountability would be ensured with a swipe of our ShipCard. The process slowed even more because one of the two crew members who'd been dealing with passengers melted away.

Had this prescient crew member seen Leah approaching? In that case, I couldn't blame him. I'd have melted away, too, if I'd had warning she'd demand I watch something of hers.

My stomach sank a little. My head said, Oh, *nasty-word* to itself. It was too early on a blue-skied, sunny day to deal with her.

Somewhere between my stomach and my head said, *Get a grip. Say yes or say no, but make it your decision.*

I turned.

First, I noticed the line behind me had disappeared. People scattered at her approach? Took off with the absent crew member?

Next, I decided I didn't care about that. I was too focused on the fact that she wasn't talking to me. She didn't even acknowledge my existence.

Yippee! said the streak of yellow down my back.

She was talking to the towel guy. She plunked a large pink bag of woven straw atop the counter.

Now I felt bad.

Doubly bad.

First, at the inherent imbalance of power between a service-providing crew member instructed to smile graciously at a passenger behaving badly. Few passengers do, but the ones who did were real stinkers.

Second, that I had not previously recognized that the guy behind the towel counter was the leader for my muster group. The same one Leah had sniped at.

I pivoted my head toward the towel guy/muster leader, whose nametag identified him as Badar.

"No, ma'am. We are not allowed to take responsibility for a passenger's belongings."

As it had been for the muster drill, his accent was distinct, but his English was clear and precise.

"Nonsense. I'm not dragging this around with me while I look for people worth talking to. Watch it." She shoved the pink tote toward him. "My tablet's in there. I'll know who to blame if it's gone."

"No, ma'am. We are not allowed to take responsibility for a passenger's belongings."

She narrowed her eyes like a gunfighter. "I thought you'd have learned a lesson after last time."

They had a history. I'd guessed as much at the muster drill. *Last time* confirmed it.

"I did learn, ma'am. I learned the proper thing to say is *No, ma'am. We are not allowed to take responsibility for a passenger's belongings.*"

"I'll see that your supervisors hear of your insolent rudeness. To-day. Now. *Then* we'll see."

"Yes, ma'am. Please call them. That is who instructed me to say we are not allowed to take responsibility for a passenger's belongings. Ma'am."

"Why, you smart-mouthed—"

She raised her cane.

I sucked in a breath and took half a step forward in instinctive preparation to grab at the cane before it could strike Badar.

He didn't move. But fire flared in his dark eyes.

Rather than bringing the cane down on him, Leah jabbed it into the air, perhaps indicating his supervisors or her pull with the big wigs or even with the big guy upstairs. "You won't get away with this. They'll hear from me. They'll all hear from me. And then you'll hear from them and you won't be so insolent."

She spun away, cane still raised—which did make me wonder how much she needed it when she could make that spin move on a ship that wasn't lurching, but also wasn't like solid ground—and started off.

"Ma'am," Badar called after her.

She spun back. Cane still raised, no sign of unsteadiness. "*What?*"

Triumph showed in her eyes and the smirking pull on her lips. She expected him to back down, to apologize.

"You forgot your bag."

She growled. Not a little noise, but a full-throated Hound of the Baskervilles growl.

She snatched at the bag one-handed, the other still holding the cane pointed straight up. The bag's weight, with a good dollop of momentum behind it, hit the side of her knee.

She stumbled.

Another automatic reach on my part. I held her arm until she turned that growl on me. I released her and stepped back. She marched away.

"Towel, miss?"

The other attendant had reappeared, even though there was no need for his services, since the line behind me hadn't yet re-formed.

"Yes, thank you. Two, please." I handed over my card. But then I stepped to the side, closer to where Badar still stood. "My name is Sheila Mackey. If you need a witness to this encounter, feel free to call on me. Or have your supervisor contact me."

"Thank you, miss. There is no need."

The words sounded hopeful, but his tone was wooden, his expression grim. He blocked me out as thoroughly as he'd blocked out Leah.

"Really, if there's any trouble—"

"There you are," Petronella said from behind me. "I found two chairs that won't get nearly as much sun as yesterday."

I wasted no time in getting into the pool.

CHAPTER TWELVE

HUNGER, PRUNING SKIN, and the need for more sunscreen drove me out of the pool and into lunch.

After we'd snaked around the various buffet stations, and to Petronella's evident dismay, I asked a young man sitting alone if we could join him. He nodded his long-haired head and smiled.

My chatting with him kept Petronella's overzealous helpfulness somewhat at bay. Presumably because she thought I needed protection from the kid, who—as the conversation revealed—was twenty-one and newly out of college.

My guardian relaxed some at that.

She would have been significantly less relaxed if she'd gathered from several terms he used and she clearly didn't understand that the farm he talked about heading to for a year's "service"—"So wholesome," she declared—was likely a marijuana operation. Also, if she'd known he played footsie with me under the table.

Initially, mild and passably innocent.

I ended it when his foot tried to bypass my knee for higher points.

Lunch over, I said I was going to the hidden spot I'd scoped out the day before and Petronella should do whatever and go wherever she wanted. She followed me with a sigh.

I refused to feel haunted.

We took the direct route from our table toward the exit, passing through the grouping of buffet islands in the middle.

Ahead of us, I saw Leah jump up with no indication that she needed that cane, leaving a table that included the rest of her group. She crashed into a tall waiter carrying a full tray of dirty dishes. She warded off the tray and used his arm to balance herself, in the process upending the tray. All its contents spilled down his front and into a glass-breaking cascade to the floor.

"Watch where you're going, idiot" she snapped, stepping clear of the mess and continuing on.

The young man stood there, agape.

"Oh, oh, dear." Petronella clucked her tongue and began picking up pieces of glass and pottery.

Two other passengers and I followed suit, with three more people from nearby tables chipping in. On the other hand, the redhead and Piper minced past as if the mess would give them the plague.

"No, no," protested the waiter. "Please, you must not get your-selves cut or dirty." His uniform looked as if it had been washed in garbage from mid-chest, down the length of the tunic the waiters wore, with a reprise around his knees.

Another waiter hurried over, handing us trays to hold our gathered flotsam. A supervisor came on the scene, directing a third waiter, "Get the mop and bucket from the utility closet." When he objected, "I don't have a pass card," she said, "It's not locked." Then to us, "Here's a trash can for that, but please, please, no need for more."

The original waiter pitched in, taking the worst of the mess.

"I can't get any dirtier," he said philosophically. To the supervisor, he added, "I have a clean uniform in my cabin. I'll go—"

"No, no," she said. "I can't spare you with lunch still going. Get a clean tunic from the supply in the closet. If no pants fit, you'll have to make do for now. We'll sort it out later."

With that she concentrated on shooing passengers away from cleanup duty, while more workers arrived.

We continued toward the exit, trailing the stained waiter, who opened a door on the left I hadn't noticed before, showing a utility closet with stacks of the disinfectant offered at every door of any place offering food, flats of water bottles, and a clothes rack of uniform pieces.

This was probably where the young bartender headed after getting splashed yesterday by Mr. Grandpa's Sailboat on the Label.

Petronella clucked and sighed over Leah's rudeness—without ever saying her name—as we used the restroom, then I led the way to the short stretch of deck beyond the indoor pool.

She heaved a confirming-her-worst suspicions sigh when opening the door revealed Leah and Wardham sitting toward the near end of the line of chairs, Maya and Ralph at the far end, and Odette in the middle.

Odette smiled at us, while the other four pretended to have their eyes closed. I took her smile as an invitation.

I sat next to her on the Maya-Ralph side and Petronella took the next chair on the other side, leaving only two between her and Wardham.

Odette and I chatted for a minute or two about the morning and the weather.

Then we all settled in.

The only sound above the wind, the creak of the chairs, and the whispers of the ship's structure, came from scraps of conversations tubed to us from the upper deck down the conduit of the stairway.

I know. I could have not listened. But we already established I'm lousy at that.

People talk, I listen.

One voice informed us—presumably along with a companion on the upper deck—precisely how bad her feet were. In not-so-glorious detail.

"It was like they wouldn't obey me. Just wouldn't obey. I tripped and fell in the hallway. Couldn't wear shoes all summer. I mean I was stuck in sandals and *gym shoes* all summer long. Can you imagine?"

Horrors.

New voices slid in... I'd been landed in the middle of an episode of medical drama. Tests, results, medications, side effects, surgeries, scars ... I only hoped they wouldn't display them to check whose was bigger...

Drifting along—on the water and in my head—I wasn't entirely sure what was said and what my brain filled in.

"…he died in Rome. But she picked up the transatlantic cruise and…"

"…with these same people?" a woman's voice asked.

"No. Though they're about interchangeable, that's how much this group was like the one she and her husband were with then. After it happened, that gang cut her out immediately."

Was that Mr. Grandpa's Sailboat on the Label? He didn't sound the same. The wind tossed some words, letting others crash to the deck.

"But … no support or sympathy when—"

The freshening breeze must have caught the voice again, carrying it away. Or else my attention was going away.

"Sympathy? No way. She was single, she was a threat to their herd, so they cut her out. She didn't seem to…. played the role well. …. trolling in the bars. Delicately, but … one snagged by the end, with help."

"Who?"

"T-bar and errand chase sonar. You and me theme and Cheese Mary now?"

That's what I heard … but I suspected the sun, the sea, and the lunch—probably mostly the lunch—had lulled me into dozing.

The voices drifted away. Or I did.

CHAPTER THIRTEEN

"**ARE YOU TRYING** to kill this husband, too, Maya? It's an epidemic and you're Typhoid Mary."

Leah's snappy voice jolted me awake, if not completely alert.

My jolt, though, wasn't anything compared to Maya's reaction. She gave a cry and dropped a plate on the deck. The sound echoed against the wall behind us.

From the scent and the little I could see between the chairs and bodies, it had been nachos. Darn. Now I craved nachos.

"You're not married to him anymore," Maya said with a failed attempt at defiance. "I am." That almost sounded like a question.

"And that'll be the death of him. Feed him the shards of that plate you clumsily broke, why don't you? They'll do him less harm than that crap you're trying to give him. Might as well pour salt down his throat."

"Be quiet, Leah." Ralph sounded more tired than angry.

"You do know your husband has high blood pressure, don't you? Or are you too busy feeling sorry for poor little Maya to ever notice anybody else?"

"He doesn't—He's fine. He said—"

"*He doesn't. He's fine. He said,*" Leah mimicked in a whine. "You've made a career of falling apart and letting men pick up the pieces. Drove poor Bruce into his gra—"

"Stop." Ralph straightened from his bent-over position where he'd been, in fact, picking up the pieces. "Shut up, Leah."

She flushed with anger. "*Me* shut up? I'm trying to save your life from her. With your blood pressure—"

"My blood pressure's been fine since our divorce."

Our divorce? He'd been married to *Leah*?

That sure seemed to be what he was saying.

I whipped my head around to her.

Her flush turned darker, uglier. "Bullshit. I know your medical history. Thirty-seven years' worth. You think I don't remember? Or do you think your lies will make me want you back? You think you can just make it up that your blood pressure's fine and I'll—"

"He's not making it up," Wardham said earnestly. "He showed me the results. His doctor—we have doctors in the same practice, you know—was over the moon about the improvement. Took him off the medication and…"

Catching Leah's glare of disdain, he wound down.

His near-whispered finale of, "Doing good, Ralph. Real good," held no conviction.

"You are an idiot." Leah didn't waste much venom on that, yet everyone looked away from Wardham.

Ralph shoved the broken dish pieces under his chair, then cupped Maya's shoulder as she continued to gulp and shudder.

"C'mon, Maya. We're going somewhere else."

As if the idea were contagious, Petronella plucked at my sleeve and whispered, "We should go."

Leah's voice easily muscled hers aside as she addressed Ralph. "Oh, yes, yes, tend to wailing Wanda. I'm surprised you're not in tears, too. That's the kind of half-baked, half a man you are. No backbone, no strength, no fight in you."

She swatted at the air in a be-gone gesture.

Perhaps that changed her focus, because she instantly said to Odette, "And *you*. What kind of stupid, crack-brained bid was that when I said two hearts? A mentally challenged child could have done better than that. *Wardham* could have done better than that."

He startled and murmured, "No, no, dearest," leaving it unclear if he meant no, he couldn't have done better or no, he wouldn't ever consider trying because he'd never play bridge with her.

"I have half a mind to drop you. Get another partner. Someone who can *really* play."

"Let's *go*." Petronella tugged harder at my sleeve.

"No, you don't, Leah," Odette said clearly. Someone gasped. Or it might have been Maya still sucking in sobs. "You have a full and complete mind. What you lack is a heart."

This time the gasps were unmistakable, Leah's the loudest.

"Possibly also a soul," Odette added judiciously.

Petronella's tugging on my arm threatened imminent dislocation.

But I wasn't budging.

If I had, I'd either be caught up in Ralph supporting Maya up the steps, his gallantry slightly marred by the pillow sticking out of her flowered tote bag he carried resembling a huge boil on his butt, or be run over by Leah stomping out with Wardham hurrying behind after getting a death glare from Leah for being half a second late in opening the door for her.

Staying put was, by far, the safer course.

Besides, Odette was still here and I hoped to get more information.

Character research, right?

CHAPTER FOURTEEN

"I SUPPOSE I shouldn't have said that." Odette didn't sound the least repentant.

She stretched in her chair, then wiggled side to side to settle more comfortably. I shifted, too, easing my prepared-to-flight-or-fight-or-save-someone-from-being-thrown-overboard muscles. Petronella remained stock still, blank.

"You don't seem too bloodied," I said to Odette.

She chuckled. "No, I'm not." She drew in a long, slow breath through her nose. "You might notice in this game of musical matrimony that I am the odd person out. The music ended and I had no chair. Or should I say no conjugal bed."

Petronella made a sound like a puppy left to sleep alone for the first time.

Odette reached across me to pat her arm. "No, no, dear. Do not think I need or deserve your sympathy."

"But you're *alone*," Petronella whined.

"When I want to be." That glint was back in her eyes. "But you should also consider that the others still run around those chairs like demented things while I eat and drink what I want, sleep when and with whomever I want, and answer to no one, having a most relaxing cruise. You could say that I'm in the privileged position of being invulnerable to Leah's arrows."

"You still partner her in bridge, even after, uh…" My brain scrambled for a tactful way to say it.

"She stole my man?" She gave that a dramatic flourish that had

Petronella's eyes widening until Odette chuckled. "Ah, well no sense breaking up a successful partnership over a man, particularly a man who has aged as Wardham has. He should be the one named Ralph, don't you think? Yes, I see you do." She gusted a sigh. "Though that partnership might be broken up now. The bridge partnership, I mean. That would be a shame. A real shame."

"Speaking of broken up... Ralph used to be married to Leah?"

Odette nodded, a grin at the corners of her mouth, but her eyes serious.

"And what was that about a husband of Maya's, uh, dying?"

All signs of humor disappeared. "Yes. Bruce. Her first husband. A genuinely good man."

Are you trying to kill this husband, too, Maya?

She sighed. "As a matter of fact, he died on this same cruise four years ago. Perhaps naturally, Maya turned to Ralph—who had been dumped by Leah days before on the same cruise—for support in the immediate aftermath. By the end of the cruise, they were a couple. As Leah and Wardham were."

"Wow. That's, uh, amazing." The flicker of her grin encouraged me. "About this game of musical matrimony...?"

"Yes?" Her eyes glinted with amusement. "Do you want to know the rules? Or want to know how to get in on the game? Though, you have an unfair advantage at your age and with your bank account. Even worse, you should have a partner to start, Sheila. Not fair to contribute nothing to the pot and only take."

I laughed along with her. "No playing for me, thank you. I wondered, though, how it started. If you'd all been cruising together for years—"

She nodded that they had been.

"—what changed?"

She lifted one shoulder. "By the time you see dominoes falling, it's too late to know what toppled the first one. We got on in Barcelona as three couples—Leah and Ralph, Maya and Bruce, Wardham and me. We disembarked in Tampa as two new couples—Leah and Wardham, Maya and Ralph—one dead man and me. Poor Bruce."

"How did he die?"

"Heart. He'd had issues for quite a while. Years. He'd lost weight and seemed to be doing much better... Poor Bruce," she said again. "It was a shock, but not a surprise if you know what I mean."

"Was there an investigation?"

"Investigation?" She sounded slightly amused, but even more uninterested. "No. Why would there be?"

I didn't answer that directly. "What was he like? Bruce—What was his last name?"

"Froster. An r after the f. Like one who frosts a cake. He truly was sweet—no pun intended."

"What did he do?"

"Oh, he was retired, like the rest of us. He'd been vice president of a local bank. It was eaten up by a large one, as many have been. At home, my little bank was swallowed up and the customer service went right into the sewer. You would not believe——But you don't want to hear about rude cashiers and ruder managers." She smiled and I wondered again what Wardham had been thinking, trading this charming woman for a harridan. "As for Bruce, he made out quite well. He refused their first buyout offer, then with old customers continuously bypassing the new regime to deal with Bruce, the higher ups increased the offer three-fold. *Then* he said yes. He loved to tell that story. Golden parachute, he called it. More like the pot of gold at the end of the rainbow. But poor Bruce only had about ten years to enjoy it. He should have had much longer."

Based on the personalities, I guessed Leah dumped Ralph for Wardham. But what if Maya's inheritance after Bruce's death lured Ralph from Leah's side?

Maya inherited it all. Nothing divided as there would be in a divorce.

That was Aunt Kit's training talking.

"Even if you didn't notice the first domino then, you must have an idea now——"

"Leah went after Wardham, if that's what you're asking. He had no idea what hit him. I could almost feel sorry for him. Almost," she repeated in a soft tone without forgiveness in it. A frown tucked between her brows. "What I go back and forth on is whether Ralph jumped free as soon as he felt the leash loosening or if Leah sensed he was pulling away and pre-empted it by grabbing Wardham."

Another possibility involving the timing hit me. "Did the shuffling of couples start before or after Bruce died?"

She looked up quickly, sucked in a breath, then let it out slowly. "Oh, you are a sharp one. Do you know, I never once considered that. As much as I've contemplated what happened in those two weeks, it never occurred to me." She regarded me with a mixture of respect and wariness.

"I didn't mean—"

"Nonsense. You were wondering if Maya and/or Ralph got Bruce out of their way. I'd say no. I suppose you must have that kind of mind in order to write such an amazing book at such a young age."

I sidestepped discussion of "my" literary legacy, along with what kind of mind I have. Had I always? Or had I learned to look for the suspicious possibilities from Aunt Kit?

"How did you become friends?"

She laughed lightly. "Do you mean what sort of masochist becomes friends with someone like Leah? She wasn't like this when we all moved into the same neighborhood around the same time. Sharp, yes, but not like this." She tipped her head. "I suppose it's like the question of frogs in hot water and why don't they jump out before it boils them—because it happens so gradually they don't notice how hot it's become. And when they do, it's too late."

"Leah doesn't talk to you the way she does to the others. Most times."

"She used to, but she wasn't as sharp as she is now." A shadow crossed Odette's face. It was gone immediately. She gave a small chuckle. "When our children were young, I remember talking to my son, who was being bullied by a much larger boy. None of our parental recommendations or wisdom provided him any benefit. But one day he came in from school and looked immeasurably happier. My first thought was that bully had moved or been disciplined, but, no. Eric said—I will never forget this—that he'd learn to be the grass instead of the trampoline."

She chuckled more, presumably at my confusion.

"I felt exactly the same way," she said. "Eric kindly explained, saying he had watched that bully in their gym class, bouncing on the trampoline, doing tricks. When the bully tried to replicate those rudimentary tricks during recess outside, he was spectacularly unsuccessful, ending up stretched out on the grass, bellowing. Eric—truly a brilliant child—said he realized he'd been being the trampoline, giving the bully more power to bounce higher in order to do his tricks. From that moment on, he'd be the lawn, standing firm and taking away the bully's energy, rather than feeding it."

"You're the lawn? Maya's the trampoline?"

"I believe my philosopher son would say so. From our earliest acquaintance, I have endeavored to never give Leah any bounce that would let her fly higher, to do greater tricks. What many people don't recognize is that when she is merely walking along on the grass, she can be quite a pleasant companion."

I'd take her word for that. Out here in the Atlantic Ocean, not a lot of grass to test that theory on.

Her profound sigh, drew me back from contemplation of the un-grasslike ocean.

"I feel rather guilty about all this."

"*You*? Why on earth would you feel guilty? Sounds like you were the wronged party."

"Oh, that," she dismissed losing a husband. "I meant the atmosphere now. We cruised together the next two years after the, ah, matrimonial rearrangement. Or should I call it matrimonial musical chairs or matrimony-go-round. Yes—" She grimaced self-deprecatingly. "—it was a trifle masochistic the first year, with the injury that recent. But it also exposed the wound to healing salt water. I am confident I healed faster because of it. The difficulty was that as I healed, Leah ... became restless."

Uh-huh. I'd bet she'd selected that last phrase after mentally deleting *began looking for a fresh victim to torment.*

"You can't feel guilty because you didn't remain a victim."

"Oh, no. You're right. I wouldn't—I *don't* feel guilty about that at all. But, you see, Ralph and Maya canceled cruising last year. Ralph, wisely, gave no reason, but I can only imagine it was because... Well, you've seen. And without them..." She sighed. "I can bear with equanimity being a fifth wheel, but a third? No. I canceled as well. Leah and Wardham cruised alone—or as a couple, I should say.

"I found to my surprise that I quite missed cruising with our group. I persuaded Ralph and Maya to come this year, convinced in my own mind that after this elapse of time, we would all have adjusted and shifted, rather than, ah, returning to old patterns."

For a split second, I thought she'd said *old partners*.

My mistake. Or had I, possibly, tapped into something in her mind?

"The old pattern is for her to pick on Maya?"

She bowed her head in acknowledgement. "And for Maya to respond as she does. Group dynamics are interesting, don't you think?"

Whether my interest was the result of people-watching training under Aunt Kit or a natural bent, I did.

"Leah doesn't pick on you because you're stronger," I said bluntly.

Odette tipped her head now, considering. "She lashes out at me over bridge, so no, I don't believe it's completely because she consciously or unconsciously views me as stronger than Maya. I would say it's because she believes she's beaten me. She took Wardham, she's won. While Maya has Ralph."

"But Leah dumped him for Wardham."

"Yes, she did."

I perked up at a slight hesitation. "You don't believe that? You think Ralph initiated the break?"

"Oh, no. I'm not saying that. Not at all. Leah went after Wardham. Leah dumped Ralph. It happened quickly, but that much is crystal clear. Though..."

Another hesitation to jump on. "Though, what?"

"It didn't occur to me until now, with you asking these questions, but... Ralph didn't resist when she dumped him. Which some might say showed his good sense." Her momentary grin evaporated. "That was certain to bother Leah. She'd have expected him to be devastated. Under no circumstances could she be happy to see him recover immediately with the bereaved Maya."

As if I heard Aunt Kit's voice in my ear, I slowly said, "She's more focused on the women than the men, even her husband?"

"Mmm. You might be on to something there," Odette said admiringly, though I had a feeling I was following rather than leading this conversation. "She is very competitive. Very. Try playing bridge against her—or with her—if you want to experience that. So, yes, it could be… Not that I'm stronger, but that she considers she's beaten me, while Maya has not been defeated. Maya is still a player because she is with Ralph."

She sat up abruptly, patted her hands lightly on her thighs, and said, "This has all been most interesting—I can see why you are such a fine writer with your insight into people—but I must be on my way." She flashed me a smile. "Mustn't be late for bridge with Leah or she might become testy."

She departed with a cheerful wave.

Testy.

Uh-huh.

CHAPTER FIFTEEN

THE NEXT THREE days we stopped at three ports, each on its own volcanic island among the Canary Islands. Eristo celebrated with towel camels on my bed.

I still heard that tune the musicians had played that I swore I knew, but couldn't identify. That unnamed earworm was the main irritant of these pleasant few days.

Either Petronella was relaxing or I was getting used to her.

We joined excursions the first two days touring islands. Seated in what the guides called motor coaches and I'd call a bus. Taking photos through windows or at the predetermined stops. Sitting among our fellow passengers.

Some of our fellow passengers.

We didn't see Odette and the Marry-Go-Rounders or Catherine and Bob or the spa girls.

We met wonderful people from all over the world, yet with a strong streak from the Midwest. Friendly, funny, and no-nonsense. Not only salt of the earth, but with a dash of pepper.

It made me so homesick that the first night I wrote a long email to my parents, musing about possibly moving back to the region. They'd love the email whenever they got it, though who knew when that would be. You guessed it, no internet.

On the tours, around the pool, playing trivia, these people were reminders of my childhood. A species that had been rare in my past fifteen years. They now seemed almost as exotic as the black-sand beaches, frozen lava fields, collapsed volcanoes, and ash-smothered landscapes outside the bus—excuse me, motor coach—windows.

And my, oh my, did I learn about cruising. These seasoned travelers talked cruising like it was fantasy football league.

What website offers the most up to date information. Which ship's limping along toward refurbishment, which one recently came out of a rehab glowing and renewed. How and when to get deals. Wait until the last minute and take what you get? Book far ahead and be locked in? Is it worth it to own stock? Are onboard credits or price reduction better value?

Best itineraries? Swear by a travel agent or go it alone? Use the cruise line for plane tickets or book your own? And then you get the truly important choices, like early or late seating for dinner, which shows to attend, the odds of winning at the casino or bridge or bingo?

If anyone sets up a scoring system, *Cruising with Experts* could sweep the seas.

I enjoyed these people a lot.

Still, by the third island, I missed Aunt Kit's narrower but deeper dives into the surroundings.

Absent her organization, I still yearned for more exposure to the natives than a solitary tour guide.

With a bit of bait and switch, I bundled Petronella off on a tour of the island of La Palma, then I walked into the port town of Santa Cruz. I wandered the streets, snapped photos of flowers and architecture, stopped at the church Christopher Columbus last prayed in before heading toward the unknown, contemplating how unanswered prayers—since his were likely for safe arrival in the East Indies—could open new worlds.

I was contemplating that unoriginal thought and vowing to close off the topic of my future for the rest of the day when I heard the name "Leah."

The speaker sounded American. I didn't recognize the female voice and, sure, there could be other Leahs around. I stepped behind a tall spinner rack of calendars featuring Canary Island sights anyway. That way I could hide if Leah was there or eavesdrop if she wasn't.

"…I'm sure it's her. I did my research and I'm positive," the voice said.

"That's fine, darling. But what are you going to do with the information?" Ralph. I was sure of it. Almost sure.

I peeked around a calendar featuring an aerial view of Teneguía volcano.

Ralph. And Maya. I suppose I hadn't recognized her voice because I'd heard it only when it was clogged with tears.

She looked a lot better when she wasn't crying.

"I want her to know that I know. She thinks she's so high and mighty. But I want her to *know*."

He sighed. "Can't you let it go? I never should have agreed to this cruise. You said you were okay with it, but—"

"I would be okay if she weren't so vicious. She's a horrible, horrible person. Do you know what she said to that poor woman who waits hand and foot on that bigshot author?"

Excuse me?

Having completely misrepresented the situation, Maya continued, "Not that Petunia or whatever her name is understood the slam when Leah said—"

"I don't know what she said and that's the way I want to keep it. You've got to stop obsessing about her. Sometimes I feel like I'm still married to the woman. That's how much you let her into our lives."

"*Let her in?* She *pushes* in. She won't stay out."

She continued on in that vein as they left the store, turning to the right. I caught a glimpse of Ralph's weary profile before they passed out of sight.

As I left my spot behind the spinner rack, I caught the expression of the man behind the counter. It needed no translation. *Crazy tourist* came through loud and clear. At least there was a twinkle in his eyes.

It was the twinkle that made me buy that volcano calendar. One of my young nephews would love it.

I had a leisurely lunch at a sidewalk café several blocks off the main street, surrounded by locals.

Maya and Ralph stayed in my head, though.

Maya, especially. And not only because of the crack about Petronella waiting on me hand and foot.

I wished I knew her makeup secret, because no sign remained of the blotchy, tear-tracked puffiness. If it looked as good on camera as it did in the harsh overhead light of the little store—

Never mind.

Old habit not yet broken.

At the end of this cruise, I wouldn't need to worry about how I looked on camera.

In fact, whatever I did in the future, avoiding TV interviews would be advisable. Being recognized as my famous author persona could be bad all around.

On the upside, even famous authors are seldom instantly recognizable by most people outside of a bookstore. Take them out of context and they walk amongst us unnoticed.

On the other hand, it might not hurt if I made a few adjustments to my appearance.

I could go back to contacts, instead of the glasses I'd worn to look older and wiser.

Let my hair return to its wild-thing curls (and frizz) instead of the sleek flat iron look of the past fifteen years.

Oh.

I sat up straight.

Without TV cameras adding ten pounds, I could have brownies again.

In fact, I should put on *more* than ten pounds to be sure I didn't look like I had on TV.

Starting tonight, I was ordering a second dessert in addition to my dessert contribution to sharing around the table.

A dessert of my very own.

This was the most cheerful view I'd had of my future since Aunt Kit sat me down to say she was retiring.

I chatted with shopkeepers as I bought a book for another nephew, a stuffed animal for my baby niece, a scarf, spare sunglasses, and lotion, then ambled back to the ship, looking forward to sharing impressions at dinner with Catherine and Bob and—yes—Petronella.

A day apart did wonders for my patience with my unchosen companion.

CHAPTER SIXTEEN

I DROPPED MY purchases in my cabin, then headed to the soft ice cream machine by the outdoor pool.

Six passengers, a family group judging by the resemblance, reached the soft ice cream ahead of me. The machine, clearly, was not familiar to them. I could have given them lessons—blindfolded and asleep, as a matter of fact—but they were having such a good time teasing each other in what sounded like Greek to me—literally Greek—that I hung back so they didn't feel rushed.

The area around the pool was sparsely populated. On this last onshore opportunity before a string of six days at sea, apparently most of the passengers had opted for day-long excursions and were still out.

It was becoming even less populated, because the Valkyries—except for Coral—had packed their totes and were heading my way in diaphanous swim coverups.

Even here, they wore high heels that forced their feet into a balle-rina's *on pointe* position. Instead of appearing delicate and light, however, they clunked loudly on the deck.

I smiled at them.

They made fragmentary eye contact, acknowledging my existence, then a series of sniffs, apparently directed at the soft ice cream machine.

I was sorely tempted to inform them of my plan to let a number of pounds roll back on.

Where the main pool narrowed to join a kiddie pool, two hot tubs sat on each side. I saw Maya and Ralph in one hot tub on the near side, with Leah and a gray-haired man I hadn't seen before in the next tub. Behind Leah, Wardham sat sideways in a deck chair next to Odette. He appeared to be trying to make quiet conversation. She read a book with no indication of paying him any attention.

A woman deposited a bag and a towel on a nearby deck chair then strode to the tubs. She climbed in to the one Leah was in with far more determination than grace. Her arm contacted the water hard enough to splash Leah, who sputtered as if in danger of drowning.

It hadn't been that big a splash, but it certainly deserved an apology.

The woman glanced at Leah, said nothing, and began upbraiding the man in German. I know enough Spanish, French, and Italian to get by, but no German beyond *guten tag, bitte,* and *danke* for good day, please, and thanks.

She didn't include any of those among her loud torrent of words, which drew attention from all around the pool and the bar at this end.

He said little, not making eye contact with her or anyone else.

Ralph and Maya were trying to pretend it wasn't happening.

I could only see Leah in quarter profile, but I guessed from her tense shoulders and focus on the woman that she was waiting for an opportunity to jump in and take over. The woman gave her no opportunity.

The man said something. The woman talked over him. He spoke more sharply, the jerk of his head indicating their audience.

She glanced around with disdain, which I thought might rocket Leah straight through the sun canopy, then blew out through pursed lips. She stood, again splashing Leah, and climbed out with no indication she was aware of anyone else around.

The man stood—without splashing—gave a small bow of his head, then followed her.

Silence reigned as they departed toward an upper deck.

"Rude." Leah said sharply as soon as they were out of sight. "Rude foreigners. Didn't even speak English."

Ah. That added to my suspicion that what bothered her the most was she couldn't effectively lambaste the woman.

"Why should they?" Maya said. "You don't speak their language, why should they speak yours? Besides, you're a foreigner here, too."

Maya wasn't as defenseless as she seemed.

Leah turned toward Maya and now I could see three-quarters of her face. "You're strange *everywhere*. You pathetic, sophomoric—"

"Sophomoric," Maya interrupted to repeat. "That's one of your favorite words in those reviews. You use it far too much, you know."

Ralph reached a hand toward her. Restraining? Supplicating? She didn't appear to see it. She was focused entirely on Leah.

Mottled red rose up Leah's chest, neck, and into her cheeks. "You stupid, ignorant—"

"Dee North of Boise, Idaho."

Leah's mouth opened. Nothing came out.

Ralph stood.

Triumphantly, Maya continued, "That's who you pretend to be when you write those horrible, horrible reviews on Amazon. A troll. That's what they call people like you. Trolls. Leah the Troll."

The last was said over Maya's shoulder, as Ralph guided her by the elbow out of their hot tub.

That broke the spell. Wardham stood and walked away. Odette pulled her hat lower and raised her book higher. People all around the deck area and bar suddenly developed deep interest in whatever gave them an excuse to look away from Leah.

Me?

I scooted around the Greek family group, whose uneaten ice cream was threatening to drip over their hands because they'd been watching the drama, filled a cone expertly and wasted no time getting out of sight.

CHAPTER SEVENTEEN

I SET UP on my balcony—luckily with a view across the harbor to the sharp-rising coastline opposite our berth—and tried to connect to the internet.

Surprise! I did. The combination of many passengers still off the ship and the early diners getting ready must be creating this opening.

Did I check my email? Respond to my assistant? Send the agent the new bio she wanted that would absolutely make the readers in Kurdistan believe I'd written *Abandon All* with them in mind?

I searched for reviews by Dee North of Boise, Idaho.

I found them. Scads of them.

The photo was Leah. So, unless someone was spoofing her, Maya had it right. Dee was Leah's pseudonym.

I started reading.

Whoa.

Maya hadn't been kidding about her being a troll.

I am sickened by these characters... Overly sexual, overactive between the sheets...

I am weary of reading sophomoric books not remotely worthy of my attention...

I require more than mundane, two-dimensional, sophomoric, drivel, tripe...

I desire nothing more than to force this so-called author to never again foist her blatherings on me. I can't believe she's stupid enough to think this sophomoric crap is readable...

Aunt Kit has long told me that reviews say far more about the reviewer than the book. Reading one review after another by Leah, a k a Dee North, I saw what she meant.

She began every sentence of every review with I. She said nothing—and I mean nothing—positive about any book. She launched personal attacks against authors. She included nothing specific about any book or why she hated it.

She was thoroughly nasty.

On impulse, I emailed Aunt Kit. No background, just asked her to look over the reviews and tell me what she thought, included a link, and asked her to text me because there was no telling how long internet service would last.

She'd become much better at text since I'd taught her how to use voice. The woman could write book upon book upon classic book, but she could not type with her thumbs. Also, first she'd have to find the text function again, because she tended not to look at her phone except to use it ... well, as a phone.

So, I didn't expect a prompt answer.

To help the process along and get her started, I texted her, too. Much easier for her to reply than initiate one.

I went back to dig more into the reviews and the internet was gone.

✧ ✧ ✧ ✧

WE DEPARTED LA Palma into a rousing sunset.

Behind us, whitewashed houses dotted up steep hillsides like ragged steps and clouds writhed around the prickly tops, blushing vibrant pink and orange.

Before us, the ocean spread toward a sky ablaze. Almost imperceptibly the ocean quenched the fire.

Reluctantly, I closed the book I'd been mostly not reading as I stared at the horizon behind, then in front of us. Time to get cleaned up for dinner.

How much of my reluctance stemmed from not wanting to disrupt the peace of sitting quietly alone watching dark slide in and how much was from anticipating unpleasant fireworks from the Marry-Go-Round table at dinner, I didn't know.

Sure, the fireworks wouldn't be directed at me, but it still wouldn't make for a convivial atmosphere.

✧   ✧   ✧   ✧

MY PHONE HUMMED as I started down the three flights of stairs from the deck where my cabin was to the dining room. I'd knocked on Petronella's door on the way past. No answer. She'd probably already left, driven by her terror of being late.

A text from Aunt Kit. As I opened it, two more quickly followed.

The first said:

See she likes old saw "This is what passes for literature these days." ... How many books can be the worst ever?

I chuckled. I'd known the multiple "worst evers" would irk Aunt Kit. I'd heard her lecture that superlatives are singular, though I suppose this reviewer might claim each surpassed the previous in worst-ness.

Reading between the lines of the second text, I could hear my great-aunt getting steamed:

Patronizing. Presumptuous. Told Jodi Picoult, John Grisham, J.K. Rowling how to write.

Told established author to keep trying "as everything gets better with practice."

Decried all romance readers as women who have nothing going for them. Hah!

In the third text, Aunt Kit's sharp eye for human nature came through:

Needs to express purported moral and intellectual superiority to authors and audiences of books she reviews.

It was like she'd met Leah.

A rush of missing Aunt Kit hit me. Missing her sharp eyes and sharp tongue. Missing her sharing them with me in a way I don't believe she'd shared them with anyone else. I wasn't her co-writer, but I was her sounding board. And she was mine.

How would that work with us no longer in the same house?

For that matter, how would anything in my life work.

A new rush hit me. Not panic—Aunt Kit didn't allow that waste of time and energy, and the habit clung—but uncertainty and drifting unmoored.

And something else…

An uneasiness I couldn't—

Another hum from the phone.

This text said: *Though she failed to use its and it's correctly.*

"Must be a good message to make you go from misty-eyed to grinning." Odette's voice brought my head up from contemplating the screen. She was at my shoulder as we reached the bottom of the stairs. "I called to you—you were ahead of me coming from our cabins—but you were so focused you never heard me."

"Hi, Odette. Our cabins are near each other?"

"Indeed." She gave her cabin number. "You have Maya and Ralph and me down the passage one way and Leah and Wardham the other. But you cannot distract me from wondering what brought such a response from you."

I tipped the screen to shield it.

Perhaps because of that movement, she added, "Ah, a man?"

Her question was light enough that I could have easily not answered.

"My great-aunt."

"Oh, yes, you live together, don't you?"

Interesting she knew that. It didn't figure in most information on the author of *Abandon All.* Not impossible to discover, but it took reading the longest, least media-glitzy articles to find, much less to remember.

"Not anymore." I heard sadness in my voice. "She's moved into a place where she can be more comfortable."

"It's difficult when that's necessary."

It took me a beat to realize she thought Aunt Kit needed help, perhaps had dementia of one form or another. The moment to correct that impression passed when she continued.

"But you surely have enough men onboard who'd be willing to send you intriguing texts, as well as anything else you'd like. The drawback being that they're mostly old enough to be your father, if not your grandfather. Goodness, some of them are old enough to be *my* father."

Petronella waved from a spot in front of the just-opening dining room doors, where the maître d' greeted everyone with a smile and a hearty "good evening."

I raised a responding hand.

Odette chuckled, "I'll join you in cutting in. Any ire from the rest of those lined up will be divided between us, swamping neither."

"We could go to the back," I muttered. The order of arrival made no difference, since tables were assigned.

"But agitation is not good for digestion."

Without pointing or nodding or otherwise indicating Petronella, her reference was clear.

"At last," Petronella sighed. "I was so afraid you'd miss dinner completely."

The line had barely started to move through the doors when there was a stir behind us.

"Let us through, let us through," came a familiar voice. It was the leader of the Valkyries. Behind her hobbled Coral on crutches and with a huge cast from her toes up to nearly her knee. It could have gone a lot higher and we still would have seen it because her dress was slit to... I don't know exactly where because I refused to check.

"Oh, you're back," crooned Petronella.

"Yeah." Coral gave no sign of recognition. She also gave no sign of interest in anyone else.

"Those awful, awful shoes," Petronella continued. "No wonder you fell."

Coral rounded on her. "Are you saying I fell because I can't walk in heels? I've been walking in heels since I was a baby. I did not fall because of my shoes." She turned her back on us to whine, "Are we ever gonna get in? This hurts, you know. I'm in *pain*."

The rest of the group followed, crowding us back.

"You. You there. Seat us immediately," one of the men ordered the maître d'.

"But..." Petronella watching the departing back of the maître d', appeared to be in more pain than Coral.

"Now, no reason to worry." Odette took Petronella's arm, while twinkling up at the head waiter. "These kind gentlemen would not let us starve."

Their following banter gave me the opportunity to text back to Aunt Kit. *Going in to dinner. More later.*

As we walked single file toward the far end of the dining room, my phone hummed. Without taking out any of the servers balancing trays, I quickly read:

Look at her history. Patterns.

CHAPTER EIGHTEEN

OUR TABLEMATES CLEANSED the palate after Leah's display at the pool.

Catherine filled us in on all the details of how Coral and her husband had been flown to the island to catch up with the cruise once doctors in Gibraltar determined the ankle was her only true injury.

"Apparently they couldn't wait to get rid of her, either," she whispered.

Coral's plaints dominated the Valkyries' table, growing louder with more drinks. Maybe she was on drugs that didn't mix well with alcohol. Maybe it was just her.

The Marry-Go-Round table was largely quiet, with Odette and Wardham carrying the conversation, without the couple from the first few nights, who had won a small table to themselves in a corner and looked happy.

For three full days and most of a fourth, I had the good fortune to be spared any live demonstration of Leah's patterns.

After La Palma, we started six straight days of cruising, otherwise known as bliss.

I know some cruisers enjoy all the activities possible on the ship.

I enjoy the lack of activities. And I'm a dynamo compared to Aunt Kit. Give the woman a sea view, a good book, and something to drink (alcoholic or not) and she was set for days. Actually, the drink was optional.

Come to think of it, so was the sea view. Though it clearly did relax her.

Heck, these days of cruising were even starting to relax Petronella.

I spent time in the pool, chatted with friends made on the excursions, read copiously, wrote long emails to Aunt Kit describing all the characters I'd encountered, somewhat shorter emails to my family skipping over all the characters I'd encountered, and enjoyed Eristo reaching new cuteness heights with his towel creatures, including an elephant and a sea turtle that made a great pillow.

The only fly in the ointment of those easy days was the unnamed earworm.

The next time I heard those musicians, I'd ask the name.

On that fourth evening of cruising, Leah appeared to be in fine spirits at dinner. No, that might be misleading, because she spent considerable time in dark contemplation of the table usually occupied by the Valkyries and their husbands. It was empty tonight, presumably they were eating at one of the specialty restaurants. But she did not snarl or snap at anyone at her table that I noticed. Oh, a few parries at the waiter, but nothing serious.

Her tablemates appeared to chat amiably around her.

As we did at our table.

Our conversation slowed our eating, as it did every night, which was fine with me.

My years with Aunt Kit reinforced a family tendency to linger. She savored a meal, especially dessert. She didn't talk about it often, but I gathered she'd had lean days—and years—early in her writing career.

This habit offered a side benefit—no backup at the elevators when we left, because the crowds had departed.

Petronella hurried ahead of me out of the dining room. She worried the wait staff might reprimand her for holding them up.

I did say cruising was starting to relax Petronella, *some*.

Bob and Catherine went one way to take in a show. Petronella and I headed for the elevators.

The banks of elevators outside the dining room were in four sets of three, forming a rectangle, with one passageway dividing them longways and a second dividing them shortways. Where the passageways intersected, Leah stood, leaning on her cane, looking toward one set of elevator doors, which were blocked from our view by the nearer set.

Her voice rose harsh and sharp.

"…better change your tune toward me fast—"

I picked up my pace to see who she was talking to. Petronella stepped in front of me, I connected with her back.

"Oh, I'm sorry. So sorry. Forgive me," Petronella nattered, covering several of Leah's angry words.

"—worst cabin onboard seems like a palace compared to a prison cell—"

Prison cell?

I took hold of Petronella's shoulders to hold her in place to get around her to the right.

"—was in your way when the cruise started, but sure wasn't when it was over."

A strangled sound, unrecognizable as male or female, much less an identity, didn't stop Leah.

"You think you're so smart, but I know what I know. You better—"

Petronella stepped to the left, directly in front of me again. "Oh dear, oh dear, oh dear. I am sorry."

"—not give me a hard time or everybody will know. Including the police."

I half shoved Petronella and got to the open area where the passageways intersected in time to see the furthest of the elevator doors sliding closed, with no hope of seeing an occupant.

Leah was the only other person visible.

"Oh, I thought that was your voice," Petronella said cheerfully to Leah as she joined us.

"I'm going to my room." Leah turned her back on us to punch a button, another elevator door opened immediately.

"Of course, of course," Petronella said. "I like to freshen up after dinner, too. Makes one feel much more…refreshed."

She spoke the last word to the closed elevator door.

Not before Leah gave me a dark glare.

CHAPTER NINETEEN

TWENTY MINUTES LATER, Petronella, refreshed by her freshening up, and I walked into the performance area at the base of the multi-deck central atrium. Nothing was being performed at the moment, an unmusical arrangement of voices grew louder and louder.

On this deck a stage area with speakers, music stands, and two chairs, backed up to a sketchy rendition of a grand stairway, flanked by angled facets of distressed mirror that reflected into each other. More mirrors covered columns. Fake stone supported the steps that curved up from either side, meeting in a sort of balcony over the stage. A single set of seven stairs led the rest of the way up to the next deck.

That stairway offered a truncated view of passengers walking past on the next deck. Short walkers close to the steps revealed themselves as high as the shoulders. Taller walkers provided views only of the legs.

The next deck up, the view down to the stage was the hole in its donut, with armchair seating surrounding the railing-guarded opening. The decks above had ever-smaller seating areas.

Upstairs was less crowded and more conducive to conversation. But Petronella wasn't the greatest conversationalist. Plus, it didn't have a bar, which this level did.

That's where I headed, with Petronella trailing, protesting she couldn't possibly have a drink.

It was hard to guess how many customers were ahead of us, because some sat on stools—permanently or temporarily while they obtained a drink? I shifted for a better angle to assess who was next in the nonlinear line.

My Veuve Clicquot supplier Jason was behind the bar.

He turned his back on the bar, but another mirror—whoever designed this space had a thing for mirrors—caught his intense expression.

Quick calculations of angles that would have gotten me a lot better grades in geometry if I'd been able to write them down rather than sense them, turned my head to where he was looking.

The gal pals from the spa and their guys.

No—another calculation that owed only a portion of its answer to geometry—he wasn't looking at the whole group. He was looking at one.

Piper. The Valkyrie with the impressive derriere, who'd been pushed into the windows by Coral.

Piper was looking right back at him. With an equally intense look.

Sending a message.

As sure as I was of that, I didn't have a clue what that message was.

And then it shut off.

Piper looked away. My gaze shot back to Jason. He looked at the bottle he was pouring. Then back to Piper. She gazed adoringly at her husband. At least the guy I thought was her husband.

As my gaze had made that return trip to Piper, it caught something else. Since Piper wasn't doing anything interesting, I let my gaze return to the snag.

Leah Treusault.

Leah and the rest of the Marry-Go-Round group occupied a half-moon of loveseats and chairs closest to the right side of the musicians' stand, currently unoccupied. The curved stairs set the stage area off from the general seating, with this grouping the closest to the performers.

One chair in the group was empty, but all the rest held the familiar people who smiled and chatted, as if no tensions or rivalries existed among them.

Except Leah.

She was watching Piper, who appeared oblivious to her attention.

Then Leah looked toward Jason.

Huh. Another geometry practitioner?

Speculation glittered in her eyes. Her mouth formed a stark smile.

Until she saw me, seeing her. The smile converted to a scowl.

Odette, apparently catching the drift of Leah's attention, started to follow it in my direction.

I smiled generally, over their heads, avoiding eye contact, then turned completely toward the bar, as if it required a concerted effort to procure a drink. Which it might at this rate.

"Hello there, Sheila," a familiar voice said from in front of me.

Ralph, standing at the bar, presumably placing an order, had greeted me. He must be their designated drink-getter.

He smiled. "Let me get you both something to drink. And come join us, young ladies. We'd have front-row seats, if this place had rows."

"Oh, thank you." Petronella's acceptance came faster than I could muster an acceptable excuse to decline. The one time her *Oh, no, I couldn't* would have come in handy and she skipped it. "I'll have a sloe gin fizz."

Still, I tried. "I'm not sure—"

Ralph closed that off with a wink. "No worries as the Aussies say. She's all sweetness and light now. With Maya, with me, with everybody. She's most likely got her zingers in to somebody else. It's like light breezes and sunshine after a hurricane. Another champagne?"

What could I say to all that except, "Yes, thank you, that would be lovely."

Jason cut off the other bartender, saying, "I'll take care of the champagne." He winked. A little too chummy for my taste.

Then I saw what he was pouring.

I'd suffer a wink for Veuve Clicquot.

I thanked him and discreetly topped up Ralph's tip.

Ralph arranged for two more chairs to be added to the grouping, then escorted us triumphantly to the others, leaving a waiter to deliver the order, except my champagne, which I held onto. "See who I persuaded to join us?"

CHAPTER TWENTY

EVERYONE CALLED OUT happy greetings as if we hadn't seen them in weeks, maybe years.

Cravenly, I maneuvered into the added chair farther from Leah. That put Petronella near her, but since my great-aunt's sort-of relative started by gushing about the older woman's spangled dress, that might go well.

Wardham, on Leah's other side, was equally attentive.

That allowed me to slip in between Odette and Ralph.

"I'm surprised to see you here. I thought Le—You all preferred the Wayfarer Bar."

Her eyes sparkled. "Is that why you came here instead?" She waved a hand to stop my response, then said cryptically, "You'll understand before long."

"I've been meaning to thank you for suggesting the camel ride. It was fun. Not something I'd ever expected to do, but I'm glad I did." I lowered my voice. "Even Petronella enjoyed it. Especially after it was over."

She, too, kept her voice low. "Then she did better than Leah. We all took the camel ride the first time we stopped at the Canary Islands, years ago now. She swore up and down that her camel purposefully made her ride uncomfortable. You know with them tied in a line the way they are there's not much a camel can do other than walk slowly, right behind the one in front, but that didn't deter her. By the end, she was fuming. She tried to hit the camel on the neck, then on the backswing, she hit the head of the one behind her—the one I was on, which the tender had said was grouchy. That knocked the cover they put over their mouths askew. We tried to warn her—" What Odette tried to do now was not laugh. "—but that made her turn around and the camel spit right in her face."

I covered my mouth to mask my laughter.

"Oh, dear, I shouldn't laugh," Odette said. "She tried to hit it with her bag and one of the men had to restrain her. The camel handlers said it was the first time one had spit in years, decades. But its aim was great. It got her right in her open mouth."

She coughed, laughed, then subsided.

As if she knew she was being talked about, Leah swung her head toward us.

I froze. Odette handled it beautifully.

"And, yes, that same acquaintance from previous cruises said more about our friends from the spa. The core group apparently has been on other cruises." She chuckled, planting the idea that our laughter might have stemmed from that topic. "I referred to them as trophy wives. To which my acquaintance said, *Trophy wives. Hah. Only if you're talking about the kind of trophy given out for finishing fifth in a summer camp relay race.*"

I chuckled to add my bit to the impression this continued the topic that made us laugh.

"Coral, the one who pushed Piper into the window, showed up a few years ago. Apparently, she's had to work hard to be part of the group."

I only half-listened.

I suspected I'd spotted why the Marry-Go-Round folks were here.

The guitarist and violinist, the same musicians from the Wayfarer Bar approached the stage, carrying their instrument cases.

I listened to Odette, but I watched the musicians. And Leah.

She watched only the musicians. One of them, anyway. The guitarist.

"But Piper has been accepted readily, even though she's only been around for less than a year. That drives Coral wild, as we saw."

The musicians set up quickly and smoothly, with the ease of practice. Their heads were close together as they spoke softly in a language

I didn't understand, but guessed was Eastern European. My second guess—that their conversation was about music—was stronger since they were setting sheet music on the stands, one in front of each of them, apparently coordinating the order of the songs.

Odette continued, "My acquaintance said she wouldn't have been surprised if Coral had pushed Piper down those stairs, but was surprised Piper was still standing and Coral wasn't."

I turned to her. "Was your friend there when Coral fell?"

"Came on the scene just after." The lines at the corners of her eyes deepened. "Retains a vivid memory of Petronella."

I bet. I returned to watching the musicians. These two musicians' voices, their looks, their movements, all screamed *couple* to me. "Piper was there when Coral fell. Were all of them?"

"Only the two of them."

I shifted my gaze to Leah without moving my head.

She watched the guitarist.

"Uh-huh," Odette said into my ear, apparently abandoning her previous topic.

That twisted me to look at her.

Her eyes glittered. "She's taken quite the interest in that young man. Because you're a nice person, you're thinking maybe she's wondering if he reminds her of a son, a nephew. Look again."

I didn't have to. I knew she was right.

I suspected the guitar player knew, too. He was careful, as they began to play, to not to look in this direction.

In contrast, the violinist took frequent, quick, worried glances toward Leah.

Despite the violinist's apparent distraction, the music was as lovely and enjoyable as it had been in the Wayfarer Bar. It was like the music from the two instruments danced together.

When the duo stood and quickly left the stage area for a break, there was a sense of blinking back to awakeness after a restful dream.

"Music soothes the savage beast," Odette murmured.

"Breast," I corrected automatically. Aunt Kit had drilled that into me, while commenting on the lamentable inaccuracies of modern education. "Sorry."

"No, no. Is it truly breast, not beast?"

With some reluctance, I said, "William Congreve. *Music hath charms to soothe a savage breast,*" I quoted. *"To soften rocks, or bend a knotted oak."*

That started us on a conversation about the plays Aunt Kit had taken me to in New York.

Before we knew it, the musicians returned.

As they settled into their seats, the polite gatherings of all nationalities in the chairs in the center quieted. Initially the crowd at the bar ranked as only marginally louder. That diverged sharply in the next minute.

Bartenders delivering drinks constantly stirred the crowd at the bar. One set left, everyone shifted, and new people arrived.

Blips of conversations bobbed up to the surface, intercut by a symphony of catarrh coughs, snorts, and sniffs.

"Frankly, I'll be more careful about where we book next time. There should be a certain elegance. Even in these days." Those words came from between the bright red lips of the leader of the spa pack.

"I know, I know," came the redhead's voice, eagerly adding its apparent disgust with the state of passenger lists nowadays. "You can't open your balcony door and not be exposed to how provincial it's become."

Hard to imagine a ship kept running by citizens of a dozen-and-a-half countries being provincial.

The red-lipsticked leader ignored her contribution. "Next time, Harve, we get the suite, like I wanted."

"Oh, the suite is lovely," popped in the redhead. "We're very comfortable there."

I turned my head in time to see the eye-dagger the leader jabbed into the redhead, who smirked a bit, but was nowhere near as impervious as she wanted to appear.

The next words came from another direction. Behind me. Male voices.

"I'm telling you, I'm sure. He wants to go back to his first wife now that she's inherited that pile of money."

Could that possibly be about Ralph? Just as Odette had told me about people from other cruises, this speaker could know the background of the Marry-Go-Rounders. Could money be the reason that group didn't kick Leah to the curb?

"Never understood why he made the jump. The current Mrs. is a piece of work."

I shifted, trying to spot these speakers without being too obvious.

"He jumped to her because she knew how to play him. Or else he had no choice, because she roped him in and that was that."

"What good's money then?"

Now that sounded more like Wardham's situation with Leah.

"He must've figured it would buy him enough cake to have it and eat it, too. You know, a little on the side."

"Or a lot on the side."

My imagination? Or was there something familiar about that voice?

The hell with subtlety. I craned my neck.

Did no good, because of the intervening and moving bodies.

"So, why didn't he?"

"Hah. Not only does he know what would happen to his crown jewels if he tried, but *she's* the one doing her best to play around. Why, I heard—"

The voice temporarily disappeared under the surface of a new shift among those at the bar, and I still hadn't pinpointed either speaker.

"He keeled over not far out of Rome. She was gone a couple days on that leg of the cruise, but rejoined for the transatlantic leg. Talk about the merry widow…"

I'd heard this before… The voice gossipy from the deck above…

I glanced toward Odette. Were they talking about Maya?

But Bruce Froster died on a cruise with the same schedule as this one and Maya stayed onboard … hadn't she?

The musicians began to play.

The conversations didn't cease, but I couldn't hear them any longer. Not to mention that turning and staring would scream that I wasn't listening to the music.

Their first song was a lilting rendition of *Wonderful World*, sharing its joy while achieving a restrained dignity.

As the last notes held, a strident voice from the other side of the seating tore across the music and the mutters of conversations from the bar area.

Leah jumped up, jabbing her cane in the air. "You," she seethed.

There might be stronger people who would resist turning to see whom she addressed. I'm not one of them.

It was the German-speaking woman from the hot tub standoff. The man from the hot tub sat next to her. He didn't look any happier than he had then. She clearly saw Leah's cane pointed at her.

She laughed loudly and harshly.

"*You*," Leah repeated. "You *barbarian*."

"*Ach du Lieber.*" The German woman turned it into a guttural sneer.

Leah's response was a higher-pitched, but equally sneering, "Bitch."

So much for a wonderful world.

In switching my focus from one woman to the other, I saw the musicians speaking earnestly to each other.

The music re-started abruptly. It was energetic and beat-driven. Nothing like I'd heard before from them as it landed somewhere between an Irish jig and flamenco. It not only drowned out the two women, it spun Leah back to the stage.

Wardham tugged her sleeve. She jerked her arm away but dropped into her chair.

Despite her husband/male companion's efforts to shush her, the German-speaking woman appeared to still be talking, based on her moving lips. But the music covered the sound.

Smart. The duo followed with several more up-tempo pieces, then shifted to their more usual fare, including the tune they'd played in the bar. My earworm. I swore I knew that title, if it would only surface.

It had lyrics, but I couldn't quite...

Darn, what was it?

The duo wrapped up to appreciative applause and put away their instruments, then music.

"They're done?" I said wistfully.

"According to the schedule," Odette confirmed. "Next up is *Follow the Leader Dance Party*."

"I'll skip that one."

"Ah, because it's not one of the nights with an extra hour?"

"Even if it were, I'd skip it."

Petronella headed out the near exit, which gave access to the ladies' room.

I stood, intending to talk to the musicians, hoping for earworm relief. Before I could, my gaze connected with the violinist's, seeing each other as people, not passenger and entertainer. I smiled. Her mouth twitched toward a small response.

Then her expression changed as she watched Leah make a beeline for the guitarist.

He shot a look from Leah to the violinist, then hurried toward the far exit to a hallway. The violinist grabbed the rest of the music into an untidy bundle and picked up her case, trailing him, but ahead of Leah.

At the doorway, Leah came even with the violinist, then lurched sideways as if the ship had rocked. I hadn't felt anything. Leah's lurch elbowed the young woman, who stumbled.

Leah shot ahead of her and was on the heels of the guitarist when they disappeared from sight.

CHAPTER TWENTY-ONE

I STARTED THE next day on my balcony.

Many cruise veterans consider a balcony a luxury they'll forego. They like to sit out in the public areas, moving around the ship depending on if they want sun or shade, less breeze or more.

I love the balcony. Of course, for the privacy. And for the ability to hear the ocean whenever you feel like opening the door—if you've bothered to close it at all.

But the biggest factor is that the opaque privacy screens on either side allow you to frame your experience as you choose. Sit one way you look back to where you've been. Switch seats and you're looking forward to where you're heading.

Look one direction and watch the gathering clouds we were sailing toward, as I had faced when I first came out here to eat my room-service breakfast. Or move to look in the other direction and see only a cloudless, blue-skied horizon, as I did now.

So what if I was looking behind me. It was a much prettier view.

The islands were days out of sight. But that horizon behind us was bright and open and ... familiar. Especially compared to the uncertain clouds ahead that could be masking anything.

You're right. I'm wimping out about looking forward to where I'm heading.

In my life and in the next half hour.

I understood the life stuff. Big changes, major course correction, uncertainty, and all that.

The next half hour was that I'd promised myself I'd take a brisk walk around the jog track for at least a mile.

Yet the buffet beckoned, much more alluring than the walk. Yes, I'd decided I could ease up on my weight restrictions as part of my disguise once I stopped being the author of *Abandon All …* or was I shedding the disguise of the past fifteen years?

Either way, I didn't want to do it all during this cruise. And all with sugar. To be blunt, the buffet bulge threatened my wardrobe.

Did I crave sweets because of my disrupted life?

Or because of displaced tension from the Marry-go-Rounders, whom I seemed destined to spend a lot of time with on this cruise. It happened that way on cruises sometimes. You saw a few people over and over, while never running into others, only to discover six months later you were on the same ship at the same time.

Yes, and there was also Petronella.

I told myself she was only trying to show her gratitude. My mother's voice in my head reminded me to be kind.

Aunt Kit's said a few different things. I always had loved that woman.

Even when she sat me down in her office in the brownstone and kicked me out of the nest.

She'd had good reasons.

"The trouble is we've become an industry. Not a cottage industry, more like a villa industry, supporting a network of people who have a vested interest in doing the same thing over and over. Agent, assistant, publicist, editor, publisher—"

"Me."

She patted my arm. "Not you. You want to move on. You just don't know it yet. And you've more than earned your keep."

Wanted to move on? Not so sure. Recognized the wisdom. Yes.

My time as hot young writer had passed its expiration date some time ago. That is, it passed for the author of *Abandon All*. Not me, Sheila.

Yeah, this got complicated sometimes.

I left the balcony and prepared for my day among the people.

Then—*boom*—I remembered the song played by the guitarist and violinist that I hadn't been able to identify. The earworm had a name.

Hey, that had to be an omen, right? It would be a good day.

THE FIRST PERSON I saw—almost as soon as I opened my cabin door—was the violinist from the musical duo.

I almost didn't recognize her.

She moved slowly along the corridor. I drew back into my doorway to let her pass, thinking she was a passenger I didn't recognize.

Taking her for a passenger was justified, because crew members found in the hallway outside the passenger cabins wore stewards' uniforms. She wore jeans and a t-shirt.

Just before she would have passed, her identity clicked in my head and I turned and spoke without checking in with the higher functioning levels of my brain.

"That song," I blurted at her, letting my cabin door close behind me.

She jolted, eyes rounding.

"The song you and your—the guitar player played during the last set. It's an Irish song called *The Fields of Athenry*."

The lyrics came rushing in along with the title. The story of a young, him in prison about to be shipped to Botany Bay for stealing corn to keep his children alive and her preparing to see her love leave forever.

Now that I'd blurted out the earworm identity, I had room to notice that, in addition to rounding, her eyes were producing tears. She was crying. And trying hard not to.

"I don't know."

"It goes kind of like this." Yes, I tried to hum. Or whatever it's called when you *da-da-dum* an approximation of a tune. In my case a distant approximation. Lamely, I ended with, "It's very pretty."

"I don't know."

She had a heavy enough accent—my Eastern European guess strengthened—that I wondered if that's all she could say or if the phrase conveyed her incomprehension of my English.

"Are you okay?" I figured that had a better chance of being understood by any non-English speaker, as long as they'd seen an American
movie or two.

She dipped her head, bringing a tissue clasped in her left hand to
her eyes. The crying made noise now.

"What's wrong?"

"Must go. Must not be here." So she spoke some English. "Must
go."

"Can I help?"

She shook her head sharply, which might have loosened some
internal lock, because she ran down the hallway, putting her right arm
out to balance against the wall now and then, while her left hand
clutched the tissue.

She paused once, halfway to the door to the Atrium area, looking
toward a door on the same side of the corridor as my cabin, then
hurrying on even faster.

When she pushed open the door at the end, I headed the opposite
direction for my virtuous walk.

CHAPTER TWENTY-TWO

I DO NOT run.

I do not jog.

I walk.

Sometimes. I've grown rather fond of town cars and limousines.

The first circuit, I didn't notice much except my muscles moving. Interesting sensation.

The second circuit, I saw a figure wrapped in towels like a mummy in the fifth-to-last deck chair on the shady side, with nobody nearby. It was breezy and still morning cool, but not *that* cold. Of course, I was moving. Virtuously.

The third circuit, I confirmed what I'd suspected the previous time I'd passed—that hair sticking out of the top of the mummy wrap, combined with the short stature made Leah a likely candidate. If being on this shady side left her so cold she had to wrap up in towels, why didn't she move to the sunny side?

Not that I'd ask. She was a champion nose-biter and I liked mine as it was.

Then I was distracted by a snippet of conversation between two men who'd been talking stock trades the previous two times they'd pass me.

This time, strider one said, "Is that legal?"

"Yeah, yeah, of course it's legal."

"But you wouldn't want everyone to know."

"Hell, no."

Prime eavesdropping.

Wishing I had a button to run that back to know what they were talking about, then speculating about their possible activities, I didn't think much about the figure on the deck chair.

Until I came around again.

The fourth circuit, with me squinting at the figure as soon as it came into sight, confirmed this mummy wasn't moving.

That could be explained. She could be asleep. Nice and cozy in her cocoon. Not wanting to be disturbed.

Just keep going. Finish this circuit and I'd have a mile in. That's what I came here for. Not to tangle with irascible Leah Treusault. Or anyone else, if it wasn't her.

I wasn't close enough to see breathing and I couldn't be sure anyway because of my own movement.

Oh, c'mon, Sheila. Stop making up stories in your head. Of course, she's breathing. Somebody would have noticed.

I slowed as I neared that chair.

Just keep going.

I slowed more. Two people huffed as they passed me. Irked or out of breath? I didn't care.

I stepped off the track and went to the deck chair. Not too close.

"Leah?"

Nothing.

Closer.

"Leah?"

Nothing.

Closer.

I touched her shoulder. Jostled it slightly.

Most of my hand encountered towel. But the tip of my index finger encountered something else. Something cool.

I pulled my hand back.

My hand had something on it.

Uh-oh.

CHAPTER TWENTY-THREE

I STARED AT a tacky, dark red smudge on my index finger.

My brain spit out *Does Not Compute* messages.

Concentrate.

Figure out this dab of dark red and the world would be okay. Sure, sure. That would do it.

Figure this out. Logically. Step by step.

I had nail polish on my nails from the spa that first day, not to mention nicely shaped ends and less visible cuticle, and you might reasonably think that made spotting red on my fingers unremarkable.

But I opted for what's known as an American tip polish. With the ends painted a less shocking white than the better-known French manicure (really, those things could be used to direct traffic at night) and clear polish over the beds of my nails. That made the red remarkable and wrong.

Strawberry preserves from breakfast? Not the right color. Plus, I'd washed my hands before leaving the cabin.

I smeared at it with the pad of my other index finger. Not the right consistency, either.

It looked like…

I brought my finger to my nose and sniffed, catching a faint, metallic scent.

…and smelled like…

Blood.

I closed my eyes and thought.

What can I say? I'm not the screaming type.

Procrastinating type, yes. Screaming, no.

Okay, also the denial type.

Instead of acting, I reviewed where I'd been since leaving my cabin.

The encounter with the violinist.

But we hadn't touched, I didn't recall any sign of blood around her, and her hands had left no trace when she's put one against the wall to balance and the other to her face to stop tears.

I'd come up the stairs, stopped at the buffet where, yes, all right, I'd picked up a cookie, maybe two, for later.

On the way in and out, I'd received the obligatory squirts of the antiseptic/antibacterial stuff they dish out by the gallon at entry and exit of each dining venue. No red on my hands.

I found a deck chair, deposited my things on it.

Again, no sign of blood.

I'd started walking.

Three and a half circuits, being passed by joggers and other walkers, then occasionally passing a greater laggard, all while making no contact with person, railing, or other object.

Except this figure whose towel-wrapped shoulder had felt … odd.

It was *not* moving.

At all.

My breath suddenly hurt my chest and throat.

No screaming, but should I call for help?

That would draw a crowd.

What if there were clues that would be obliterated?

Clues to what?

Not going to think about that right now.

Not.

Going.

To.

I turned my head, watching the intermittent stream of joggers and walkers. Unfortunately, from where I stood and with the direction they were moving, I saw their backs after they'd passed me.

As I stood there, not recognizing anyone's back, a thought crept in.

Not precisely about what I was not thinking about, but close to it.

Some people I might spot would not be good choices to call over to this towel-wrapped figure because of possible, uh, conflicts of interest. Assuming someone was responsible for the person who might be Leah no longer breathing.

That's blood on your finger, toots. People who stop breathing in their sleep seldom have blood on their shoulders.

That voice in my head was getting old. If Aunt Kit had wanted to come along on this cruise, she could have darned well come instead of hitchhiking in my brain.

After a few minutes of standing stock still, watching unknown backs stream past, I would have accepted even the individual who had the absolute biggest conflict of interest. In other words, whoever might be responsible for nothing under the towels moving.

No, maybe not.

Besides, how would I *know* that person was the one with the biggest conflict of interest. And he or she might do something that prevented the, uh, conflict of interest from ever being exposed and then I'd be responsible for someone getting away with—

"Bob!"

Not a screamer, but I'm a hefty shouter and that shout turned several heads around ... including the one my brain had recognized and communicated to my mouth to shout to while the rest of my mental power dithered about *conflict of interest.*

He peeled away from the flow of joggers and runners, curling back toward me.

"What's wrong, Sheila?"

Where did I start?

Not by saying aloud the question drumming in my head:

Did Maya finally crack?

CHAPTER TWENTY-FOUR

I'VE BEEN ON a number of cruises and somebody dying during one isn't unheard of, especially on the longer ones. You pack a few thousand people who are more Boomers-and-Beyond than Millennials on a ship for a week or two and the numbers will tilt that way.

This death, however, was from decidedly unnatural causes.

The blood on my hand was the major clue.

She hadn't just been killed. Crack of dawn exercises were held on this deck even before the joggers and walkers started. They might not notice a non-breathing figure, but they'd notice someone depositing it in a deck chair, not to mention someone killing and wrapping a person in towels. So she'd been put here a while ago. And she hadn't put herself here.

Which led to the strongest point: How could she have ended up wrapped in towels if it was a natural death?

Apparently, the ship's officers called in by Bob agreed.

They quickly blocked off that part of the deck, escorting all passengers except Bob and me and whoever was in the towels well away from the activity.

They also used a tarp to mask the area from prying eyes. Though the wind confounded those efforts a few times.

My eyes pried for all they were worth.

I also eavesdropped on conversations between the medical personnel and ship officials.

From those, I knew the blood I'd encountered wasn't the cause of death. I mean blood usually isn't a cause of death in itself, unless you lose too much of it, which would have created a scene no jogger could have missed.

"Stabbed?" the first official with stripes on his uniform asked the doctor.

"I'm no pathologist, but I don't think so. Certainly not fatally. More likely a skin tear when she was, well, I suppose you'd say strangled."

"What do you mean, you suppose I'd say strangled?"

"It appears, from the lack of markings on the back of her neck, that something was held across the front long enough and hard enough to kill her."

Before I heard more, another official with fewer stripes on his uniform started asking me questions.

After questions from a sequence of ship officials, I was escorted down several decks, into an interior warren of narrow hallways and tiny, utilitarian offices not meant for passengers' eyes.

Up ahead, I caught sight of Wardham being ushered into a room by another official. When we reached the door it was closed, showing the sign: Chief Security Officer.

I was led two doors farther, then invited to enter. As I passed the long title on the door, I caught the name Henri Lipke and something about passenger satisfaction. I had the better end of this than Wardham, assuming Henri Lipke lived up to his title.

Rising from behind his desk to greet me, Lipke displayed a Clark Gable in *Gone with the Wind* mustache with no other resemblance to Clark Gable. He was short and thin. He smiled smoothly, then remembered the seriousness of the matter and grew solemn with disconcerting speed. He had not been among the officials at the scene.

Assuming this was being recorded, I supplied my name and submitted to his questions with the best grace I could muster with a major headache knock, knock, knocking.

No, I hadn't met the victim before this cruise. No, we didn't spend *a lot* of time together. No, I hadn't liked her. No, I'd never killed someone I didn't like—he didn't ask that question. I threw in the answer for free.

"Tell to me again what reason you possessed to stop to check on your friend?"

"Not my friend," I repeated. "Acquaintance. I met her through a fellow passenger. In the spa the first day—"

"In the spa," he murmured, not sounding happy. Death—even if it wasn't murder—was not good for passenger satisfaction.

"Yes. We were having manicures."

"You and the deceased passenger?"

"No. A different woman." I felt oddly reluctant to share Odette's name, though surely Wardham would tell the Chief Security Officer about the group traveling together. And all the currents and cross-currents among them. "That woman and I hit it off. She later introduced me to her friend, Leah Treusault. That is the woman I found."

I rubbed at my forehead, as if friction would cure my headache.

Repeating my story was getting old.

Lucky me to discover the victim.

All those people passing me on my circuits must have been going too fast to notice the towel-wrapped figure's complete lack of movement.

They said the murderer often returned to the scene of the crime. Could this one have returned over and over while circling the track? Keeping an eye on the victim while keeping fit? Murderous multitasking?

Henri Lipke made a note of what I said, even though I'd said it before. I kept my questions and speculations to myself.

He looked up through his lashes while keeping his head down. "And your companion? Ms. Domterni?"

I gave him a hard look. I was fair game. I had found the body. Petronella was Bambi, Peter Rabbit, and a few other defenseless woodland creatures rolled into one. Sure, some might say her brain power fell into the same range as those woodland creatures, but she was family by Aunt Kit's standards.

"She is not my companion in either the old European sense nor in the current sense of partner or significant other. She is a sort of distant relation." I was not explaining to this man how Aunt Kit's long-dead fiancé figured in. "And she not only wouldn't hurt a fly, she would pick the fly up after someone else swatted it and give it a decent burial. Sure, you've got to consider me when you write up your list of suspects, but forget—"

"Suspects?" His eyes bugged out in dismay. "For a natural death?"

"I don't think so." I gave it a touch of the satirical sing-song intonation where you go up on the *think*. It felt good. Like a normal person, instead of a vaunted author. "Blood, remember? I suppose that might be natural, but from the doctor's expression when he unwrapped her from the towel—" I restrained myself from repeating *I don't think so*. No sense rubbing it in and making an enemy of him. I might need help with my passenger satisfaction later. "—probably not."

"How did you—? You were not to see. The passengers were to be shielded, the covering to protect them from the ugliness."

"The crew did its best, but the wind caught a corner of the tarp."

That wind-arranged gap had momentarily revealed a flash of red where Leah's shoulder and neck met, along with an impression of something wrong with her throat. And that was before hearing the doctor.

"Not natural," I said with confidence.

His eyes dropped. Bingo.

"That brings us to suspects," I added.

"No, no. I do not think—"

I held up my hand. "Her husband." Index finger raised. "Her ex-husband." Middle finger. "Her husband's ex-wife." Ring finger. "Her ex-husband's current wife." Little finger.

"You must not say such things."

"Wait. There's more." I waggled my thumb. "A German woman Leah clashed with."

"No, no, no. Not on the Diversion."

I wasn't done. "Also, she made herself unpopular with a number of the crew, including the woman who plays the violin so beautifully with the guitar player."

"Anya and Pyorte." He still looked unhappy but not as deeply disturbed.

"Then there was something nasty with the towel guy. And if she'd treated me the way she did any of the waiters, I'd have been tempted to pop her."

Though I wouldn't have killed her. On the other hand, I could get away from her. They were stuck serving her—food, drinks, towels— day after day. Sometimes cruise after cruise, too. And having to be nice while doing it.

"Ah," he said with deep meaning. "The towels. Such as wrapped her. It must be one who hands the towels to passengers who did this."

"I thought you said not on the Diversion?"

He spread his hands wide. "If it must be, better crew than a guest." His mouth turned down, but he lifted one shoulder slightly in fatalistic acceptance. "What name was this person you saw be nasty with her?"

Badar, the towel guy, wasn't my favorite, but that didn't mean I'd vote to have him railroaded, especially since anyone could have snagged towels.

"Not him being nasty. Her. *She* was nasty to *him*." I shook my head, slow but sure. "Sorry. I don't remember a name."

"What description did he have?"

More head-shaking. "I don't remember. I was focused on how nasty Leah was being."

"She was this *nasty* to you?"

"I never took a direct hit. Just caught in the general miasma of her nastiness."

Including whoever she'd been talking to at the elevator last night, making noises about a prison cell. Hyperbole? Or did she know something? That person seemed more likely to have been a passenger than a crew member, considering crew rarely used those elevators. But—

Henri Lipke interrupted my speculations by asking, "Your companion?"

I didn't answer immediately.

He didn't meet my eyes. He understood English well enough that he hadn't stumbled at *direct hit* or *miasma*. Yet he'd used unusual constructions and he'd repeated that identifier for Petronella that I'd objected to.

Uh-huh. My buttons were being pushed.

Slowly, I said, "Ditto. Same as me."

He didn't blink over that or seem to have any issue understanding.

Instead, he said, "Tell me again, starting from when you began to walk the track."

His English had improved radically.

CHAPTER TWENTY-FIVE

LIPKE EXCUSED HIMSELF "for a moment" that turned into more like forty-five. Long enough to realize that with *The Fields of Athenry* identified, a new earworm had taken up residence.

T-bar and errand chase sonar. You and me theme and Cheese Mary now.

The nonsense syllables that were the last thing I'd heard from the gossiper on the upper deck early in the cruise.

What on earth did they mean and why did they haunt me?

When he returned, they at least—and at last—served me lunch.

That helped my headache. But it didn't go away completely as we had yet another round of Same Old Questions.

Finally, he politely thanked me for my time and sent me on my way.

It was after three p.m. Five hours since I found her.

I wanted fresh air and solitude.

I headed for my cabin, specifically the balcony.

On the way, I realized the death was the only topic of the snatches of conversation I heard. Though no one identified me—yet—as the body finder.

Walking to the elevator…

"The cruise line'll try to keep the death hush-hush. They all do it. Discreet, anyway. They sure don't want to advertise that someone's croaked during their cruise…"

"I heard there'll be a burial at sea."

"Nah. They have a morgue to hold bodies until we get to a port."

In the elevator…

"You know they have cameras all over. They must have security video."

"They could see it was a waiter who left the body there—"

The hair on the back of my neck stood up. They had *video*.

At least according to rumor.

"—but didn't know which one…"

"How could they not know which one if they had video? The person covered his or her face? Then how did they know it was a waiter?"

Good questions.

Wish I knew the answers.

Outside the elevator…

"I wonder if the heirs get a partial refund."

"Why would they? It's not the cruise line's fault this person didn't finish the trip."

"Unless the food killed them. Or a fall in the bathroom or—"

"How could anyone fall in a bathroom? They're so small, you could *try* to keel over and still be found standing up."

I closed the door between the public area and the corridor where my cabin was, cutting off the voices.

With my key ready to open my door, I heard a male voice.

"Oh, miss. Horrible for you to be the one who…" It was Eristo, my cabin steward. He usually left towel creatures on the bed for me, now he offered condolences on finding a body and proving the crew grapevine was faster than the passenger version. "Can I do anything for you? Something you require? I left the ice in your refrigerator. Anything else, I would be happy…"

His brown eyes shone with sympathy. And something else.

"Thank you, Eristo. That's kind of you. If I think of anything… But right now, I'd like to…" I tipped my head toward my cabin door.

"Yes, yes, yes. Such an awful thing for you to find. All the questions. For you. For others."

He spread his palm to hold the door open for me once I'd unlocked it. I stepped in. Before he could withdraw, I faced him.

"Eristo, you said others were asked questions. Do you know

who?"

"Oh, miss. I should not." He looked up and down the hall.

"Of course, of course." I backed up, through the narrow hallway between the bathroom and closet, back until I felt the bed behind me, then I sidled to the side. "There was one thing I hoped you might help me with. My, uh, suitcase. Getting my suitcase down from the shelf in the closet."

"Of course, miss." He came in, letting the hall door shut. He made no move toward the closet.

"Under normal circumstances I know you would never share information with a passenger." I held his gaze. "But this is not a normal circumstance, is it?"

"No, miss."

"If you're not comfortable telling me who's being questioned officially, tell me what is being talked about among the crew."

"Ah. Well. The crew, we see much more. The officers—" He flicked a hand. "—they occupy themselves with *important* duties, too important to notice. The staff, too. But we, of the crew, we are with the guests far more."

I'd gotten the distinction between the officers and the rest, but... "I'm sorry, Eristo, I don't understand who's crew and who's staff. I thought everyone was part of the crew."

He scoffed at that with a discreet snort. "Those who give the shows, who sell in the shops and such, say they are staff. We who care for the guests are crew. Stewards, waiters, cleaners, bartenders—" His expression told me something important was coming. "—those who offer the towels."

I treaded carefully. "You know all these people? The bartenders, the waiters, the people who offer towels?"

"Many I know. Often not well, but a little. Some I know well."

I thought about the musicians. Anya and Pyorte, Henri Lipke had called them. But according to Eristo, they were staff, while he was crew.

Those who offer the towels. Had I imagined his emphasis?

I didn't want to jump right in with Badar, but I couldn't think of anyone else, and I'd already waited too long. The opening would close—

I blurted, "Do you know Jason? The bartender Jason?"

His shoulders dropped slightly. Relaxing. Talking about Jason didn't worry him. Perhaps that's why he said, "His head cannot get through many doors."

I puffed out a brief, surprised laugh. "I suspected that." With the atmosphere lighter, I went for it. "What about Badar?"

"A bartender?" He was buying time.

"No. He is not a bartender. Not that I know of, anyway. He gives out towels."

"Ah." He looked down at his hands. I waited. Footsteps sounded in the hallway. Eristo tightened. They passed the door unchecked and a layer of his tension eased. He breathed out through his nose. "He is off his duties now. He has been asked to talk to the Chief Security Officer." Another pause. "Since more than two hours."

About the time I mentioned a run-in between a towel guy and Leah to Henri Lipke, even though I hadn't mentioned the name. How had they known? I wondered if anyone else was answering questions. For instance, members of the Marry-Go-Round group beyond Wardham. Or the musician couple.

Unaware of my wondering, Eristo continued, "One who does know him is a friend of my girlfriend. She is a good woman, even though she is staff. She works in the spa. You know her, maybe?"

My brain was a beat slow. Maybe I knew his girlfriend? Or Badar's girlfriend? "I don't think—"

"You have, I see, a manicure from the spa?"

"Yes, but—"

"Maybe you need improvement on your manicure? Fixes. Need to see her again. Sit with her right there, close to you. Easy to talk then."

Imka?

Tentatively, I said, "That could be a nice break for me after all the questions I've answered."

He nodded encouragingly.

"The woman who did my nails before was wonderful. Imka. That was her name. Imka from South Africa."

"Yes, she is nice lady." He gave me an intense look. "She has someone she cares about. A member of the crew. He has hot head sometimes. He says things sometimes, things not good to say. To guests. To officers. Imka says this is only because he is smart and feels things strong."

Ah. She'd fallen for a Mr. Tactful.

Didn't need a pricking in my thumbs to guess *which* Mr. Tactful.

"Imka's boyfriend is Badar, who works at the towel desk?"

Eristo went on alert. I didn't think I'd said anything remarkable. He'd made it darned clear.

Then I, too, heard what sounded like footsteps coming to a stop by my door.

He might have good reason for being cagey in what he said to me, since I knew from other cruises that fraternizing with the passengers was strictly against the rules for crew—and staff.

I raised my voice. "Yes, thank you for that suggestion, Eristo. That does sound good. I'll see if I can get a spa appointment—"

"I am sure miss can have time with this woman who does nails in—" He looked at his electronic watch. "—ten minutes."

"Great." I dropped to a whisper. "But how did Imka know you're my steward—?"

He kept his voice low, too. "There are many connections in the crew. We know many things."

That was a bit scary, but I'd worry about that later. Back to full voice. "I guess I better get up there then. I'll …" I gestured toward the bathroom.

He immediately backed to the hall door. "Yes, miss. If you want me to bring down your suitcase?"

"No, thank you. I've, uh, changed my mind."

"Yes, miss." Then, with more emphasis. "Thank you, miss."

✧   ✧   ✧   ✧

FOUR MINUTES LATER, I was on my way to the spa, without even opening the door to the balcony for that dose of fresh air I sorely needed.

Working backward from the breadcrumbs Eristo had left, Imka wanted to talk to me. She'd either known or found out that Eristo was steward for my cabin. She or her friend, Eristo's girlfriend, asked him to get me up to the spa.

Imka and Badar. Really? She could do better. She was smarter, kinder, and more personable. Probably not the time to say that to her.

But why did she want to talk to me?

First possibility was the grapevine had filled her in and she'd pummel me for hinting at Badar, even without using his name. The better scenario was she thought I could do something to help.

I was afraid I'd disappoint her there. There was a big gap between brainstorming how to approach a mystery Aunt Kit made up and trying to unravel the real thing.

Besides, if I were a real sleuth, I should talk to Badar directly.

Although that might be out of the question. Chances were, the Chief Security Officer had him fully occupied. Even if they weren't talking to him, they likely had him somewhere a passenger couldn't wander into and start chatting. Besides, would he want to talk to me? Even if he didn't know my comments led to his being questioned. On top of all of that, what on earth would I ask him?

For that matter, what would I talk to Imka about?

I didn't know anything about real investigations.

Yes, you do, Aunt Kit said in my head. *You took to it like a duck to water when you started helping me with my mysteries.*

I didn't have to imagine those words. Just remember them from the numerous times she'd said them.

"Okay. I'll do it like we're in the brownstone."

The words calmed me. Unfortunately, I said them aloud in the elevator as it took me to the spa deck and I wasn't alone. I received wary looks from two robust, white-haired ladies, who let me go first, with plenty of space between us.

CHAPTER TWENTY-SIX

IMKA MUST HAVE been watching for me, because she came to the reception desk the instant I arrived. Her smile was broad, but worry dimmed her eyes.

"Oh, miss, you glow. A man?"

More like extra desserts. Or... was I glowing from interest in a murder? That wasn't very nice. Had to be the desserts.

"No man." I smiled, not mentioning double desserts. "I'm hoping you might be available to freshen up my manicure. I have a chip." I fisted my hand so the receptionist couldn't see its chipless state.

"I am free now—"

"Excellent." I beamed at the receptionist, then took Imka's limp arm and led her into the nearest little room, closing the door behind us.

"What's wrong, Imka?"

"Nothing, nothing wrong. What can I do for miss today?" she said brightly, but she slumped to the stool in the corner and tears dripped from her closed eyes.

"Didn't you want to talk—?"

Her anxious look toward the door stopped me. It was the same reaction as Eristo.

Would her fellow employee rat her out to the officers for talking to me? On the other hand, did it matter if the woman *really* would? As long as Imka worried about it, she wouldn't talk openly.

I pulled out my phone, found what I wanted, cranked up the volume on my Christmas playlist, left the phone on a counter near the door, then joined Imka on the other side of the room. Only four feet separated us from the door, but with our heads close together and the wall of sound between us and the door, we couldn't be overheard.

If I could get Imka to talk.

I barely stopped myself from humming *The Little Drummer Boy.*

"It's safe now. Tell me why you wanted me to come here."

"That woman. That woman ... you found her? Dead?" She spoke hesitantly, but she was talking.

"Yes."

"Was she... Could it be an accident? Or suicide?"

"I don't think so."

She chewed on her bottom lip.

I let the silence expand.

Finally, with a huff of breath, she said, "I have a boyfriend, a *serious* boyfriend, no matter what some say." She tossed a glare in the direction of the reception desk, providing a clue about who might say that. "He is smart and he *feels* things, you know?"

Almost the same thing Eristo had said. Gee, wonder where he'd heard it.

"You are smart. Everyone says so. And famous." She gripped my arm. "You help him? You can help him? Please?"

"Help him? How?"

"They accuse that he did this thing. They believe he—You know. The lady you found when no one else did. On the deck."

I couldn't say it was a great surprise. Not after Eristo. Still, it was another thing to have it right in my face.

The ship's officials suspected Badar of murdering Leah.

Even without naming him, I'd provided his possible motive. (Clearly, Imka didn't know I was their source for that tidbit. I hoped she didn't find out.)

And now Imka wanted me to help clear him.

Gulp.

"Why do you think they suspect your friend?"

"They ask him questions and questions and questions. They ask where he was each second. I know he cannot say."

"Sure. It's hard to account for your whereabouts every second."

"He knows. He cannot say." She emphasized the second sentence.

Great. He was hiding something. That did not bode well for Imka's romantic future with this guy. "To protect you? If the two of you were together—?"

"No, no. We were not. It is his honor he protects."

"His honor? He told you—?"

"When we first heard about the dead woman, before they took him for questions, he told me he has sworn to tell no one. It is not his secret, he said. He would not tell me. He will not tell the officers."

"But if he has an alibi—If he can prove where he was when they think she was killed, he could—"

"He will not."

She said it with such finality, even a shade of pride, that it effectively blocked that avenue.

I shuffled what I knew at this instant and tried again. "If all they were doing was questioning him—"

"So long."

"—you can't get too worked up about that, Imka. They'll ask a lot of questions of a lot of people. That's how these things work." That sounded confident. As if I knew from personal experience, rather than from books and tagging along with Aunt Kit on research gigs.

"Yes?"

"Yes."

What I didn't say was that I knew things the officials would be interested in hearing and which might make Badar look more guilty. Like the details of the exchange over the towels and the indication it wasn't their first clash.

My instinct had been to not share that, but maybe I should. Maybe it was wrong to keep things from the officials investigating.

Aunt Kit's voice in my head snorted disdain for that idea.

Yeah, Kit, but dealing with a real murder...

She snorted again.

Well... I didn't have to make a decision about giving the officials details right this minute.

"Imka, you can help Badar by telling me the truth." I stifled an *If he's innocent*.

"I tell you the truth, but how does it help my Badar?" she asked.

"To find who did this and remove all suspicion from Badar. Hiding things will cause confusion, even suspicion." I paused a moment. "You might not want to be real open with your bosses. I understand that. Crew—People working on the ship knew Leah from other cruises, didn't they?" She remained wary, no smile in her lovely eyes. "*The she-devil's onboard.*"

She recognized the words. It flickered in her eyes.

"Your bosses already know, don't they? They know the crew, the staff—like all you here at the spa—consider Leah Treusault the *she-devil*. Can it hurt to tell me?"

"She was not a nice woman, not a kind woman."

"That's true."

"She was on the ship a year ago."

"I know. Did something happen involving her?"

"With that one? Always."

When she seemed to stall there, I asked, "Like with Badar."

"*No. Not* like Badar. She tried to make that other ... *do* things. You know. Man and woman things. He was young. He was new steward. Didn't know how to handle a passenger. He ran out, made a big deal. They gave him different cabins, gave her and her man a different steward. Someone old. Someone who knew.

"But she kept after that first one, trying to find him, trying to catch him in other cabins. He left after. Said the money is not worth a crazy person like that."

Did Pyorte, the guitar player feel that way, too? Or had he found a different solution to Leah's unwelcomed pursuit?

Suddenly, Imka said vehemently, "It's not like they say. That he hates her. Because of the other times she is on the ship." Ah, the officials already knew there'd been previous conflict between Badar and Leah. That lifted that burden off me at the same time I felt unreasonably irked that others knew what I'd thought was my discovery. "He does not like many, many of the passengers like her who come often and oft—"

Dismay clouded her eyes as she heard her words.

I leaned closer, put my hand on her arm. "I know. Lots of people didn't like her. She wasn't nice. Not to a lot of people. And you—crew and staff—had to take it. But you're right, that doesn't mean he killed her." I extended what she'd said. "His not liking a number of the passengers, including repeat passengers, doesn't mean he killed her, either, because then a lot more people would be dead. Logical?"

Her eyes widened, then slowly nodded.

"What happened when Badar met that passenger—Leah—before?"

She gave an elaborate shrug. "Nothing. She's not nice, but that is how she is." Another shrug. This one would-be philosophical.

"What dealings had you had with her before?"

"I do her nails once. She is not happy. I feel bad to start. But she is not happy ever. Not with anyone in the spa. Maybe not with anyone on the ship."

That sounded right. But wasn't new information.

"Tell me when you last talked to Badar."

"This morning. After they—you found that woman. We pass for a moment on I-95 and—"

"I-95?"

Her mouth flickered toward her usual smile. "It is what they call the main hallway where many cross paths, much comes in and goes out, all below the passengers, without you ever knowing."

"Okay. You ran into each other and had a minute to talk, what did he say?"

She spread her hands. "There is little to tell. We both say we have heard that news. He says he heard who the passenger was who died. He says he cannot say where he was last, but we don't talk long."

I sat back a little, drumming my finger in time to *Joy to the World*.

"I saw him giving out towels yesterday afternoon. Do you know what he did after that?"

Apparently glad to contribute, she said, "When the pool closed, Badar stayed to close the towel stand. He stored the clean towels. He carried the used towels to the laundry, as he always does. I saw him, then, for two minutes, three minutes, four minutes. No more. Then I return to here. He has short time to eat, because he has next to offer drinks to guests who do the dancing on the deck by the pool."

Serving drinks to the passengers…

I heard they could see it was a waiter, but not which one…

And Badar had been a waiter last night.

Wait. How could the officials know it was a waiter on CCTV if they couldn't recognize the person?

Oh. Right. Had to be. How slow was I? They could tell the person wore a waiter's tunic.

I found a small smile for Imka. "Yes, the waiters look handsome in those tunics."

Her smile showed. "He does, my Badar."

"Those tunics are kept behind the bar?"

She shook her head. "No room there. They are in a closet across the way from the bar."

The utility closet by the buffet.

After Leah trashed that waiter, I'd noticed plenty of other crew members going in and out of it. Not even needing pass cards, because it was left open. Anyone could have slipped in there.

Badar had a tunic. But anyone else could obtain one, too.

"That's helpful. See, you know what goes on onboard. You must know a lot about what goes on between the passengers … and others."

Her worry instantly deepened. She said nothing.

"Imka, what did Leah—the woman who was killed—do to Badar?"

"It is not motive. I know what you look for and it is not," she said anxiously. "This woman she threaten many, many of crew, of staff, even of officers that she will have us fired. She says this all the time. One, two, maybe she has pushed when they were already on the edge, like the steward. You understand?" I nodded. "But not to end Badar's contract right that minute. No. No, she could not do such a thing."

Maybe, maybe not.

Did Badar think she could? That was the important element.

"She told him that on this cruise?"

"On this cruise, on one before, and one even before that, before I was here to calm him. But saying it many times does not make it so."

Not only was she right about that, but her account raised a factor in Badar's favor. If Leah had been threatening to have him fired across three cruises and it hadn't happened, why would he suddenly think it might happen this time?

Certainly took the edge off his motive.

CHAPTER TWENTY-SEVEN

"SHEILA!"

Catherine came toward me along the exterior walkway beside the indoor pool. I waited for her to reach me.

I'd wrapped up with Imka after the receptionist knocked on the door and asked with unconvincing meekness when Imka might be available to take an appointment. The receptionist also stared suspiciously at the lack of equipment in sight.

"All set," I said cheerily. I splayed my fingers and raised my hands. "Imka did a beautiful job, didn't she? You can hardly tell where she made the fix."

Under my breath, I murmured to Imka that I'd be in touch and told her to text me if something else came up, while I pressed a tip into her hand with my cell number on it. I held it so my thumb pointed to the numbers. She'd seen it.

Turning off the music, I nattered to the receptionist about how much I loved getting into the Christmas spirit early. The suspicious woman accompanied me out past the desk and beyond the confines of the spa.

I'd barely shaken her off when Catherine appeared.

"You are the talk of the ship," she said.

"Great," I grumbled.

"Only good is being said about you. How calm you were. How you kept your head."

"I was screaming on the inside," I admitted with a grim smile.

"I'm sure, dear. But what matters is what you did on the outside.

Bob was impressed by you."

"I'm grateful he answered my shout and got the officials."

"They kept you such a long time. You and that woman's husband. Who, apparently has been spinning a tale of marital sweetness and light, even though he also says she never returned to their cabin last night."

"No."

"Yes. He says he fell asleep and didn't wake until they came to find him this morning. And only realized then that she had not slept there."

"They suspect—?"

She shrugged in slow-mo. "Though, even if they don't, I under-stand why they kept him. They needed time to search their cabin for any clues."

"Is that where she was killed?"

As I asked, I recognized I had full confidence Catherine would know. She did not disappoint.

"No outward sign of it. No sign of a struggle or blood or such. They have now moved him to another cabin, allowing him only the fewest personal items from their luggage and checking it all quite thoroughly, whilst they have supplied him with toiletries and such from the shops. They even had the doctor inspect all their prescriptions—his and hers—before allowing him to take his regular medications."

"How do you find out all this stuff?"

She waved that off as trivial. "What I don't understand is why they kept you so long when they believe they know who did it."

"The killer often is the one who finds the body. Not this time. I swear—"

"Ach, I never doubted it." I'd never heard her sound more Scot-tish. I was touched that strong feelings about my innocence brought it out.

"What do you mean they believe they know who did it?"

"They have video from those closed-circuit cameras around the ship. But I understand the quality's not what one would hope."

"Then why do they think they know who killed Leah?"

"Because, they say, that grouchy young man giving out the towels is the only one with a motive. Because Wardham's been telling them that not only he, but everyone loved Leah."

"But I told—" I broke off, realizing announcing I'd pointed out a bunch of people with potential motive might not make me popular. Not that Catherine would blab, but things could slip out—I looked around—or be overheard.

She nodded agreement with my unspoken belief that there were lots of potential suspects. "But the officers investigating appear to be full speed ahead with one view. Nice and neat. All wrapped up. Turn it over to the authorities as done and dusted when we next dock."

"But that's... That's the day after *tomorrow*." We were scheduled to cruise tomorrow, then spend the next day on a Bahamas beach used exclusively by the cruise line. We'd leave there in time for dinner, sail one full day, then arrive in Tampa early the next. "Can't they wait until we get to Tampa?"

"Can or can't, they aren't going to."

"That's not—" I hesitated over the final word to swallow down the what-am-I-getting-myself-into foreboding that rose in my throat. "—right."

She took me by the arm and turned me toward the elevators. "It's not. It's not at all right. So, get about your work."

"Me?"

"You help your great-aunt with solutions to her made-up murders. Apply that here." It was like a Scottish echo of Aunt Kit.

"How do you—"

"Petronella told us of how your great-aunt has been a not very successful writer for so long and you've helped her."

"That's not—"

She pushed me on my way.

CHAPTER TWENTY-EIGHT

"**MADAM**," **HENRI LIPKE** started, patient but weary.

Not letting him get a head of steam, I interrupted. "You need to hear what I have to say." I'd fought like crazy to get through layers of crew, staff, officers, or whoever else tried to stop me seeing him and I didn't intend to be shut down now.

"Perhaps later—"

"Let us hear the passenger," said a soft-spoken man with a barrel chest and broad shoulders, appearing in the hallway behind him.

Lipke sighed but made a small bow, acquiescing.

The newcomer said, "You are, I believe, the person who found our unfortunate victim?"

"Yes. Shall we sit somewhere? This might take a while."

"Let us, by all means, become comfortable," he said. "I am Gerard Edgars, the head of security."

The guy who'd talked to Wardham.

Also, I'd seen him up on the deck, near the body. He'd appeared to brief the captain at one point. He never spoke loudly enough for me to hear anything he'd said there.

"Then you'll be interested in this, since the word on the street—or ship in this case—is that you're relying on CCTV footage showing—"

"Passenger rumors are not—"

"Let us listen, Henri," suggested the Chief Security Officer.

Smart. Shipboard rumors could be, might very well be, wrong. But what was being said gave an insight.

"Thank you. As I was saying, the rumor is that you're looking at

CCTV that shows a crew member. Specifically a crew member in a waiter's tunic. That's why you want to hear this—among several things I need to tell you. A few days ago, one of the excellent waiters in the buffet had the misfortune to be bowled over—" Blinks told me that hadn't translated well. "He was run into by the woman I found, Leah Treusault. She came away unscathed. He had all the contents of a tray of dirty dishes he'd collected poured down the front of his uniform. A supervisor and two other waiters came over to help him, along with passengers." I modestly omitted that I was one. "Though not the instigator of the crash."

"Who is this waiter?" Henri demanded, as if prepared to add the name immediately to a list of prime suspects.

I held up a "wait" hand. "His uniform was past saving. He said he would return to his cabin for a clean one. The supervisor said she couldn't spare him, but he could get a clean tunic from the utility closet and make do with his pants. Clean uniforms were kept there for such emergencies. And it was not locked."

They got it immediately.

Henri's face fell.

The head of security closed his eyes a moment. When they opened, he asked, "Who heard this conversation."

"A good number of people. All the workers who helped clean up. The passengers who helped clean up. And passengers seated nearby, including all of the dead woman's party. As you'll be able to see from the CCTV of the buffet that day." After a pause, I added, "And of course, everyone any of those people told."

NOW HENRI CLOSED his eyes. "Everyone."

"Lots of crew and passengers, anyway," I said cheerfully.

He groaned.

"But you don't have to worry about everyone. Oh, everyone might have heard about the episode, even know about the tunics in the closet, but that still doesn't mean you have to consider everyone a suspect. A few can be ruled out. Anyone legitimately in a wheelchair, for instance. A few are physically too big to have been the figure in the grainy video image. That eliminates any NBA players who happen to—"

"How do you know the size—?"

"Must be about average or you wouldn't be zeroing in on Badar."

"How do you know grainy—?"

"Immaterial, Henri," murmured the security chief. "What else, Ms. Mackey?"

"If you could see someone clearly, you wouldn't still be looking at suspects," I told Henri before I answered Edgars' question. "Perhaps a few people on board can also be eliminated as too small," I mused. "Though carrying her would not have been that difficult for anyone of any size as long as they had the strength to get her up over their shoulder into a fireman's carry."

"In theory."

"But you aren't going to consider *all* the possibilities, at least not yet, because your experience has told you that the closer the person was to the victim, the more likely he or she is to be involved. It's best to start there."

"Closer to the victim, yes. Also closer to the incident," he said smoothly. "So let us begin with you, Ms. Mackey."

"You aren't really interested in me or you would have questioned me yourself already, but okay."

I went through my account yet again. It had a sing-song quality by the end. "…so that should reassure you that I didn't have anything to do with killing her, because why would I find her body, especially so fast. She could have been there hours before Wardham reported her missing. Longer time before discovery usually makes the investigation harder."

Edgars' blink acknowledged my point about Wardham, whether his failure to act stemmed from guilt or ineffectualness.

"My innocence," I added, "must be a relief because my name would call even more attention to there being a murder on the Diversion."

Lipke winced. Edgars didn't. He continued to regard me.

"Do you have experience in law enforcement, Ms. Mackey?" Of

course, he used my *Abandon All* name.

Which, I realized was a benefit to this being my public swan song as that persona. The media would pick up on *Abandon All*'s author finding a murdered woman. I'd be inundated … if I weren't already withdrawing from public life.

"No, and I think you know that. Though my great-aunt and I have attended many classes, workshops, and behind-the-scenes tours because she writes mysteries."

"I see. Is there anything more, Ms. Mackey?"

Oh, hell yes. And I wouldn't let his disapproval and/or dismissal stop me.

I repeated what I'd told Henri about the Marry-Go-Rounds, the Valkyries and their consorts, and the German woman, adding more detail because he was a receptive audience.

Once, he looked away from me to send a reproving look toward his colleague, who expostulated, "But he—the husband—told you all was good, how loved she was. With such tears he said it."

Gerard Edgars continued to look at him. Henri subsided.

I concentrated on presenting my information calmly, coherently, and factually to the security chief.

When I stopped, taking a long drink of water, he asked, "What were your observations of the victim."

"In an Agatha Christie novel, she would have been the family despot attended by a long-suffering and dowdy daughter, a seedy middle-aged son who drank too much, an aged and poor relation who served as a companion, and other period satellites.

"Modern times being what they are, she was accompanied by her husband and that was it. He seemed happy enough, showed no sign of drinking to greater excess than his companions, and I sure hoped he wasn't related to his wife."

He didn't comment, but again asked politely, "Is there anything more, Ms. Mackey?"

Some stuff was so nebulous it made what I had told him sound like slam-dunk-and-slam-the-cell-door proof. "Not that I can think of now."

"*Bon.* We thank you for your observations."

He asked no follow-up questions, but I'd given him plenty to spread suspicion well beyond Badar. They couldn't just dump Badar in the Bahamas saying "He did it." If they left all the possibilities and witnesses there, they'd have a real hole in their passenger list. Surely, they'd take everybody on to Tampa.

Which would give ... somebody ... time to keep trying to unravel this.

I looked at Edgars for a sign my take was correct.

His eyes were flinty.

Pretty sure that was for Henri and for the situation. Though some might have been for the messenger, who looked a lot like me.

CHAPTER TWENTY-NINE

MY MIND WAS on Badar as I started climbing the stairs toward my deck to wash up before dinner.

What if he *had* done it and I'd distracted them with tales about petty, domestic unpleasantness?

Badar had easy access to the tunics. He could have carried Leah. He had opportunity.

Who didn't fit all those?

As I'd pointed out, only the extremes of big and small could be eliminated. Also, whoever had been steering the ship that night. Though, for all I knew, the ship had cruise control and he could have dashed out, done Leah in, then gotten back to the helm.

I rubbed my forehead.

Okay, that was a stretch.

But the video hardly eliminated anybody as a suspect.

Among those not eliminated? Badar.

On the other hand, if Edgars had been sure about him, they wouldn't have listened to me. So, something held the security chief back even before I pointed out the wide-open access to tunics.

Did he consider Badar's motive weak, agreeing with Imka?

Leah raising her cane straight up as she snapped at Badar...

How physically threatening had she truly been? Badar could have held her off one-handed.

Plus, as unpleasant as Leah could be, she wasn't the first annoying passenger he'd dealt with, even repeat offenders. Besides, his response at the muster had been to stay away from her. He might have been angrier after the confrontation at the towel counter, but he'd kept his cool then, too.

Getting him fired seemed a stretch, as Imka said. Edgars didn't strike me as overly impressed by—

I stopped climbing steps.

It took another two beats for my conscious thoughts to catch up and realize why I'd stopped.

Another time Leah had raised her cane. Not threatening as she had with Badar ... Not overtly threatening...

I looked up at the open risers a full flight above me. There wasn't much space between them from this angle.

Turning my head, I looked across and up at the next half-flight of stairs. This allowed considerably more latitude. Someone on one half-flight had an open view through the openings to the next half-flight.

"What are you doing, Sheila?" Before I could answer or divert Petronella, she knelt on the stair where I stood. "Oh, you dropped something, you poor thing. And after the horrible trauma you've experienced. Let me help you look. What did you lose?"

Dropped?

But I was looking *up*.

She hadn't waited for an answer. She slid her hands across the carpeted stair as if she could find an individual grain of sand if that's what I required.

"I didn't lose—"

"Oh, dear," came another voice. Maya Russell. She hurried to Petronella. "Are you all right? Did you fall? These stairs can be so dangerous. You know a young woman fell at the beginning of the trip? That's who they dropped off in Gibraltar, though she was healed enough to rejoin at Gran Canaria. Why they had to make that side trip when she was fine three days later except for that cast on her foot, I don't know. Especially when those young women wear those outrageous shoes. It's a wonder they don't all break their necks. Not that I'd wish that on anyone. Especially after Leah—"

Ralph Russell stayed back, watching us.

Maya hiccupped from swallowing what might have been a sob. Or a laugh.

Jumbled emotions following the death of a long-time friend? Or something else?

Are you trying to kill this husband, too, Maya?

"Maya, I want to say I'm sorry about the loss of Leah. I know you had... difficulties, but you'd known her so long and so well."

"We weren't that close."

"No, but... You'd cruised many times together. And to have someone else you knew die on a cruise must bring up feelings and memories—"

"We better go, Maya." Ralph, standing between us, had a hand under her arm, urging her up. "It's been a difficult day. Sure you understand."

They were gone before I could even glimpse her face.

Four more people had joined us. Three gallant men from sixty to at least ninety and another woman.

All scoured the steps.

If I didn't supply some object for their search, one of these canny folks might figure out what I *had* been doing ... if Ralph hadn't already.

Could Leah's ex-husband know about—

Focus. I needed to focus.

"I dropped an earring," I blurted. Automatically, I put a hand to my earring-less left ear, which matched my earring-less right ear. "Earlier. I got to my cabin, took one off and realized the other was gone."

Not great, but better.

We all bent over searching the carpet. I got bored fast, knowing we were looking for something that wasn't there.

I looked around at the shoes passing us. What else was there to do?

Running shoes in white, black, beige, one pair of red. Two pairs of practical black sandals. A tiny pair of white sandals that reminded me of some I'd had as a kid. Petronella's practical close-toed flats. One pair of sandals. Four inches, but steady with a steadying wedge, unlike—

Shoes. Stairs. A cane ... A cane stuck through the opening, even for an instant—as long as it was the right instant—would trip anyone. Especially anyone wearing absurdly high-heeled sandals.

But why?

Had Leah encountered Coral before?

That confrontation outside the elevator last night...

...Better change your tune toward me fast—

—worst cabin onboard seems like a palace compared to a prison cell—

—was in your way when the cruise started, but sure wasn't when it was over.

Had Leah tried to get rid of Coral, then threatened her ... only to have the other woman kill her?

If so, Leah knew some secret about Coral. But—

I jerked upright.

"What is it, Sheila?" Petronella grasped my arm. "Are you dizzy? Sick? Faint?"

"What? No. I'm fine. I, uh... maybe the earring's in the pocket of what I was wearing before. No sense anybody looking more until I make sure. Thank you all for your help."

I thanked more, they said I was welcome more, while Petronella fretted about my emotional state.

What actually straightened me up was realizing the security video did eliminate one person. Someone wearing a cast that would be impossible to miss even in grainy footage.

In a millisecond Coral spun from hot suspect as the probable victim of Leah's cane trick, to eliminated. Maybe I *was* a little faint.

CHAPTER THIRTY

DINNER WAS STRANGE.

Quieter in one way with the Marry-Go-Rounds' table empty. Though the Valkyries and guys indulged in their usual boisterous drinking and eating.

The overall turnout was lower than most nights, but many found a reason to stop by our table and try to find out what it feels like to find a dead woman.

Bob fended off most with able assistance from Catherine. She called the head waiter over. After a whispered exchange, he stood subtle guard.

Once again, we were among the last to leave. Tempting music came from the atrium stage, past the banks of elevators. The guitarist and violinist—Pyorte and Anya, I now knew—were playing again.

"Good many people in there," Bob said, from his advanced scouting position.

I ducked in, enough to see he was right. Also enough to catch sight of someone walking past on the next level up. The opening for the stairs revealed only the bottom third of the female, wearing a skirt like one Odette had worn to dinner last week. But that was unlikely, since the Marry-Go-Rounders appeared to be mostly staying in their cabins.

I grimaced over the crowd, not wanting more questions about finding Leah.

"Upstairs?" Catherine suggested. We all agreed.

Petronella's seat was the only one with a view down to the stage area, which was fine with me. Listening to the music eased tightness between my shoulder blades. My eyes closed. No distractions.

Relaxation evaporated in an atmospheric disturbance as Petronella flailed next to me. My eyes popped open. "What?"

"I don't—I couldn't—A mistake, must be a mistake." As if blown back by a blast, she was splayed in the upholstered chair.

"What must be?"

Catherine and Bob craned forward, looking over the railing. Catherine looked back at me and shook her head that she had no information.

"What happened, Petronella?"

"I... I don't know."

"You must know."

"There was a man. Going toward the elevators. I know he held up his hand. Like he was waving?"

Why was she asking me? "Someone waved to you?"

"Oh, *no*, not to me."

"Who was waving?"

"I couldn't be sure. But the way he looked..." She clasped both hands to her heart.

"How *did* he look?" Catherine asked.

"Oh, no, I couldn't possibly..."

Open-ended questions didn't work on Petronella. We needed to narrow this down.

"Drunk?"

Head shake. "Though he held a bottle of wine, I think."

"Angry?"

Head shake

"Happy?"

"Maybe. He ... smiled." She gave a small shudder. "Like a pirate."

"Bloodthirsty?" Bob asked with relish.

Petronella shrank deeper into her chair. Her hands now clutched the material over her heart.

To pull her back from the brink of considering bloodthirsty pirates' smiles, I asked, "Why couldn't you be sure who it was?"

"Oh, didn't I tell you? He was upside down."

"Upside…?"

"The mirrors," Bob said. "Must be the angle."

Catherine and I leaned over and saw what he meant. Mirrored planes tipped in such a way that people reflected upside down.

I shifted around for different angles.

Upside down and … backward. Sort of. Looking in one mirror, you saw the reflection of a reflection. As I watched, people advanced and retreated, sometimes the same person appearing to do both at the same time.

I focused on one upside down figure, waiting for her to come out by the elevators. She didn't.

She'd been going the opposite direction. Heading toward the part of the ship where cabins lined the passageways.

Had the man Petronella seen been doing the same? Or had she been looking at a single reflection?

And what the heck did it matter?

After that, we were unanimous in making it an early night, even though it was one of the time-change nights, which meant an extra hour of sleep.

As Aunt Kit said, one of the true joys of these western-bound transatlantic cruises.

After getting ready for bed, I tried reading for a while, but found my mind returning to Leah.

Pulling out my phone, I sent Aunt Kit a stream of texts about finding Leah and what I knew of the investigation.

While I waited in hopes she'd answer immediately, I re-read her texts from yesterday.

Twice.

By the end of the second time through, I knew there'd be no rapid response tonight.

Then I had an inspiration.

I tried the internet.

It worked.

Forget those warnings about pre-bed screens, I was making internet hay while most of my fellow passengers slept.

Skipping email again, I went directly to the reviews written by Leah under the name Dee North.

Look at her history. Patterns. Aunt Kit had written.

As I scrolled deeper into Dee North's reviewing history, I saw that over the past six months she rated nothing higher than two stars, while the past two months were all one-stars. Before six months ago, she'd had more twos, an occasional three, and even a four. Then, rolling back further in her history, revealed another, deep dip into vitriol and all one-stars.

I went to the start and scrolled backward through the history again, jotting dates for the one-star extravaganza periods, bracketing the times when the nastiness was more virulent than usual.

I saw a pattern.

The darkest periods came a little less than four and a half years ago, a little less than one and a half years ago, and for the four months leading up to this month.

After each of those first periods came a break with no reviews at all, then an interval where she became relatively benign.

The breaks were from late October to mid-November. Exactly the timing of this cruise. It appeared the pattern was a virulent patch, cruise, honeymoon period, before the nastiness ramped up again.

The break four years ago coincided with the great spouse swap.

But what about the break a year ago? That's when she and Wardham cruised without the others.

The cycle from relatively benign for the month or two after last year's cruise to the nastiest of all reviews before this one had accelerated from previous cycles.

I wrote an email to Kit asking if that was the pattern she'd meant, as well as recounting more of what I'd seen and heard.

Who knew when I'd get an answer. Maybe when we reached land. I flopped back in the desk chair.

What was I doing, anyway?

The Diversion's Chief Security Officer struck me as a very capable man.

On the other hand, you have access and insights he can't ever have.

That was Aunt Kit's voice. Great. No texts or emails, but plenty of direct delivery into my head.

Do you know what I'd give to be in your shoes? At the center of a real murder investigation, seeing it all from the inside? You better stay involved. I expect a blow-by-blow account and I'll have opinions on everything.

I wrapped my light robe around me and went on the balcony, enjoying the sea-dampened breeze pushing at me. The ocean was rougher tonight, the rocking of the ship more pronounced. I found it soothing.

My chin rested atop my folded arms settled along the railing, I looked out to darkness pitted by the stars and their reflections into immeasurable depth that contradictorily seemed close enough to scoop up by the handfuls.

When my chin slid of my arms I knew it was time to get into bed.

Where I dreamed of ups and downs of nastiness, ebbings and flowings of vitriol, all in time to the rocking ship.

CHAPTER THIRTY-ONE

HEADING FOR BREAKFAST, I opened my door to the hallway and nearly screamed.

Petronella stood right in front of me, her face a frozen mask as she looked down the hallway.

"Petronella? What's the matter?"

"Wh—? It doesn't make sense."

The murder? Not yet it didn't. But that didn't mean it wouldn't. Maybe, even, that I'd make sense of it.

Petronella, however, did not look as if she had confidence in that. More like she had heartburn.

I leaned out and turned my head to see what she was looking at. A door well down the hallway toward the front of the ship slid closed.

"Did you see someone? Who?"

"I wasn't sure," she mumbled. "It's strange. Like last night."

"But you must have seen—"

"He came out for a second, then he turned back and... and *kissed* her. And... Oh, he wore his clothes from yesterday." She jerked her head from side to side. "No, no, no. We won't speak of it. I came to be with you because after the horrors you faced yesterday, you need support, protection. Then... Then I saw." She fluttered both hands in the direction of that closed door. "But, it couldn't be—Because, you know."

Know? Not even a glimmer.

"Petronella—?"

The cabin door that had closed a moment before, opened and a man came out, propelled by a woman's hands. Not in anger, but determination, and with a mix of emphatic words and chuckles. They were too far down the hall to make out the words.

But not too far to recognize the people.

Wardham.

Odette.

He wore his clothes from yesterday, Petronella had said. But they weren't the clothes he'd had on when he entered the security chief's door.

Odette wore a negligee. An honest to goodness negligee with lace straps and—

I shook my head. Dislodging irrelevant details.

I grabbed Petronella and yanked her inside.

"Wha—?"

"Shh."

I closed the door—quietly, not alerting them they'd been spotted—with us inside.

"But that was... was... In *her* cabin. But ... Why?"

I wasn't getting into that.

"How do you know those are the clothes Wardham wore yesterday? When did you see him?"

"I... I don't know.

"Was Wardham who you saw in the mirrors last night with the pirate smile?"

"I don't kn—"

"You *must* have recognized him. Even upside down. Was it Wardham?"

Her hands covered her mouth, but she nodded.

Had he gone straight to Odette's cabin from when Petronella saw him last night, with a bottle of wine, waving, and smiling like a pirate? And *had* I recognized Odette's skirt? It was a straight shot to the front of the ship, then the secondary stairway and a short walk to Odette's cabin. At that hour they'd be unlikely to be seen.

However Wardham got there, he was with Odette this morning, not yet twenty-four hours after his wife was discovered murdered. He was wearing last night's clothes. She was in a negligee. There'd been kissing—heaven knows Petronella wouldn't make that up.

The other woman. Classic motive for murder, anyone? The twist was this time the other woman was the ex-wife.

He wants to go back to his first wife now that she's inherited that pile of money.

He jumped because she had gobs more money before that inheritance came in. Or else he had no choice, because she roped him in and that was that.

The roping could fit Leah and Wardham.

Had Odette inherited money since their divorce? That would mean the motive daily double—the other woman and money.

But could someone as ineffectual as Wardham pull off a murder? Unless he wasn't as ineffectual as he seemed.

Or.

He was not the brains behind the crime.

I eased out a long breath. "Let's keep this between us, Petronella."

"I would never—*never*—talk about this to anyone."

✧ ✧ ✧ ✧

I CONSUMED BREAKFAST, apparently making appropriate responses to Petronella at the table for two the maître d' kindly procured for us, but my brain was elsewhere.

It kept repeating, *Odette is so nice.*

I considered that. Did her astringency disqualify her from niceness? Possibly with a lot of people. I liked her all the more for it.

Aunt Kit's voice sounded in my head. *Your liking someone does not preclude that individual from being a murderer.*

She'd proved that in mystery after mystery she'd written in the years we'd lived together. I swear she did it on purpose. Though whether she decided a character was the murderer after she realized I liked the character or whether she made the murderer likable from the start or whether she used both methods, I hadn't yet pinned down.

I might have a better grasp on why she did it.

She thought I was naïve about people.

She had some cause for that.

I wondered sometimes if Aunt Kit's people-watching was entirely about creating fictional characters or if some of it was intended as a post-graduate course for me. If so, I was grateful, because it sure beat the trial by fire learning method.

Back to Odette.

She *was* nice. With just enough lemon to be entertaining.

That doesn't mean she didn't kill Leah Treusault. Approach this rationally. Aunt Kit's voice was nearly as bossy as the rest of her.

Didn't mean she wasn't right.

I sighed. As I ate a chocolate brioche, I asked myself what I knew that could count as suspicious against Odette.

Answers came all too easily.

Odette was the reason they were all here. She'd said as much herself. There'd been no group cruise last year, but she'd brought them together this year.

Leah had stolen her husband.

Odette hadn't said it that dramatically, but that's what it amounted to.

Plus, Odette had been the source for all my information about Maya and Ralph beyond my observations. How much of my instant suspicion of Maya was from observation and how much from Odette's take.

But Leah dumped him for Wardham.

Even so, that wouldn't mean she'd be ready to see him recover immediately with the bereaved Maya.

Was that the moment I'd started wondering if Maya's first husband might have met with foul play?

Or was it when Leah asked if Maya was trying to kill another husband?

Oh, you are a sharp one. Do you know, I never once considered that.

Was that true? Or had Odette skillfully led me to that point?

She considers she's beaten me.

Not that Leah *had* beaten her by taking Wardham away. But that Leah considered it that way.

Because to Odette the contest wasn't over?

Because Odette had been playing a different—and more final—game?

Petronella's voice penetrated before an answer to that vital question surfaced.

"Did you hear me, Sheila?"

"Uh-huh." I must have heard her in order to respond. Even though I didn't know what she'd said.

"I'm glad you agree. I don't want to be rude in saying you look tired, but a nice nap and a quiet morning—or even the whole day—in your cabin will be the best thing for you. I'm going to do the same thing."

"That's a great idea," I said enthusiastically.

It was a great idea—for Petronella. Not for me.

Once she was in her cabin, I continued down the hallway, turning toward the front stairway to get out of her line of sight if she happened to poke her head out.

With that danger past, I paused.

Imka.

She had more to tell me. I was sure of it.

You might be wondering why I didn't confront Odette.

I wasn't ready. I needed time. Or nerve. Or both.

CHAPTER THIRTY-TWO

"CAN YOU BELIEVE it? Another chip."

The receptionist couldn't believe it. But with no one else lined up for a nail appointment, she couldn't stop Imka from escorting me to the private room.

I set up the phone, playing *Carol of the Bells*.

"Badar is still held." Tears stood in her eyes.

"Imka, I can't promise you I can help him. But I will try to find out more about what happened. If he didn't do anything wrong—"

"He didn't, he didn't."

"—then finding out what happened *will* help him." My brain was churning with what to ask first, how to approach it. A Vulcan mind meld sure would save time. "But to do that, I need to know many other things."

"What things?" As eager as she was to help Badar, I heard caution.

"Remember when I was in here getting my nails done and a group of women came in? Tell me about those women."

A flash of something crossed her face. "They have nothing to do with my Badar."

An unwelcomed thought came to me: Just how protective was Imka of Badar?

She knew where the tunics were kept. Likely knew the right time to slip in and get one, too.

She had the strength to kill Leah. And to carry her to that deck chair.

Her handling of Petronella alone showed that and then she'd

pulled Piper from the windows with no evidence of strain.

"Maybe not, but, remember, I said the only way I can help him is to find out what happened. The only way *you* can help him is to help me. If you don't want to—"

"No, no. I want to help him. I must. I'll tell you."

"As long as it's the truth. It won't help if it's not the truth."

She bobbed her head.

"Good. Tell me about them." I left it wide open to see what she came up with on her own.

She frowned, speaking carefully. "They come to the spa every day. They have many demands. Sometimes they want all to be together. Sometimes all alone. The one—you saw—she leads. Always. They talk one to the other. Not to us. They do not tip."

"What do they talk about to each other?"

She shook her head slightly. "Many things. So many things. Often I don't want to hear."

"It might be important, Imka."

"I try." She went silent, her bright eyes unfocused with concentration. "They talk much of how to get gifts from their husbands. How to value them. They tell each other, too, how to hide such gifts and other—" She looked at me. "Values?"

"Valuables?"

"Yes, yes. Valuables. In a box the husbands do not know about. Stash, they say. They talk and talk about this. How best to do this. They talk also about the husbands' health." Her brows drew down sharply. "Not for caring." She released a short sigh. "But not to do anything. No action. Wishing, I think, but no action."

"The woman named Coral, the one who pushed the other lady into the window and later tripped on the stairs, does she join them here?"

"Now, yes. After she fell and even the first day, second day after she returned, not then. They say she sleeps in her cabin."

"Were they concerned about her?"

"No. This one or that one wants her appointment. That is all."

"Uh-huh. How about when she started coming, too?"

She tipped her head. "She complains often. Pain, she says. Also what she cannot do. They have no patience with that. They tell her she will lose her husband. I think they do not want to hear her themselves."

Well spotted, Imka.

"Do you ever see her moving around in a way that might make you think she isn't hurt as badly as she says?"

"Some complain if a nail file brushes the skin. Others, you could cut off flesh and they would not. She is the first kind."

"I see what you're saying. I wondered if her injury doesn't restrict her as much as she indicates. If she can move around more than she shows?"

"Faking it?" Imka asked.

"In a way. That's what I was wondering."

"But doctors—on the ship, at that hospital all see her. How could she fool them?"

That was a good question, but not insurmountable. She could have lied about her level of pain, which would contribute to their diagnosis and treatment. She could have vamped at least one into cooperating with her if she was faking it. Or she could have driven the medical staff to the point of accepting her exaggeration to get her out of their hair.

I went for something less complicated.

"You see things other people don't."

She nodded. "I say her pain is not so great as she says. But if she could, she would keep together with the others when they walk too fast for her."

Well spotted again. "That's an excellent point, Imka."

"Also, she would wear the heels. She is not happy with the shoe she must wear to make it even with the cast. She says it makes her leg look like a sausage." Her smile flashed. "And Miss—the lady she push into the window agrees, it does look like a sausage, which makes the lady with the leg very, very angry. Her face is red. The others, they talk of her. When she is not here, they do. Not when she is here."

"They talk about Coral? The one with the leg?"

"No. When she was not here, they did not talk of her at all. She did not exist. Or they forget her. I mean the ... the other. The one who was pushed into the window by the lady with the leg. They do not forget her when she is not here."

"Piper?"

"Yes, yes, I believe that is what she is called. Miss Piper." She spoke cautiously.

"What do they say about her?"

"She has not been with them a long time. She makes the leader worry. Dark hair? Red lipstick? Tall? She does not want the others to follow this Piper. She says often that she is new, is pushy, is different from them. Thinks she's clever." That last sentence came out as a creditable imitation of the leader's voice. "Also, the woman of the red hair. She worries about this new lady. But… yes, I think it is a different worry from the dark-haired lady."

"In what way?"

She paused, then shook her head. "I cannot say. I feel it, but the right words aren't here. Even in my head, in my language."

Remembering the redhead's interactions with Jason the bartender and, later, his exchange of intent stares with Piper, I pushed a bit. I might be putting words in her mouth, but maybe she needed those words.

"Would you say, Imka, that it was a more personal worry? That the leader is worried Piper might threaten her leadership, but the redhead-ed woman worries that Piper threatens something else of hers? Something personal, close to her heart?

The young woman took her time, thinking through what I'd asked. "Yes. That is so."

I nodded, satisfied. "If you hear these women saying anything else that you believe might help me…"

"They are here now."

"Here? In the spa?"

"Yes. Can that help you show Badar did not do this?"

"It might." Though taking them on en masse was more than daunting. Before she could pursue her agenda, I added, "You said Badar could not say where he was the night before last. He has to, Imka. He can't keep it from the ship's officers.

"He says he will keep it only to himself. That he must. His honor demands this."

She was a surrogate brick wall on behalf of Badar's honor that I wasn't getting through. How about around?

"Who are his friends among the rest of the crew?"

"Friends?" she repeated doubtfully. "I am his friend."

"How about guys? Does he hang around with any guys? Maybe some of the bartenders?"

"He knows Constantine, who is at the bar by the pool. They eat lunch together many days."

"Okay. I'll talk to Constantine. Anybody else? I thought I heard Badar knows bartenders." She began to shake her head slowly. "What about Jason, who works in the Wayfarer Bar a lot, sometimes at the Atrium bar?"

She stopped for a beat, then shook her head more vigorously. "Badar does not eat lunch with him. Talk to Constantine. He is roommate with Badar."

CHAPTER THIRTY-THREE

FOUR OF THE Valkyries occupied chaises in the glass-enclosed Relaxation Room at the back of the ship—Coral, Piper, the redhead, and the leader. That meant one was missing. Possibly having a treatment.

I took a chair at the end of the line and pulled out a magazine I'd found in the miniature closet they called the ship's library.

After saying she'd let me know how to find Constantine when she knew his schedule, Imka had re-polished one of my nails to have something to show the receptionist and even though the new polish was dry, I held the magazine as if it weren't.

I held up the magazine, masking my face. But I could still see the row of feet. All wearing killer-high sandals, except Coral, whose cast-less foot was bare, though still holding that ballet *on pointe* shape of her habitual shoes.

"That's the one who found the body," Coral said in a stage whisper.

So much for invisibly eavesdropping.

Not to be upstaged, the leader said, with an ennui that left me surprised she could summon the energy to speak, "It would have been a lot more exciting if that old lady had been pushed off the rock wall or something like that."

"Too much security there," the redhead said matter-of-factly.

"What security?" the leader asked, snapped out of her role as Camille on her deathbed.

"There's security all over. Well, not all over. There are gaps, but I heard they shoot up the women's shorts," the redhead said.

"No," gasped Piper. Judging by their faces, she expressed shock for them all. Forget murder, *this* was serious.

"*There* you are. At last," the leader said.

I peeked over the top of the magazine to see the fifth member of their group arrive.

"It wasn't even all that wonderful," whined the woman I would forevermore think of as The Other One. "A bunch of hot rocks. C'mon, let's go. Maybe something will be interesting today."

"Where are you going?" Coral demanded. "It'll take me longer, but—"

"You can't expect us to stay here all day. We're going to the pool. Meeting the boys—"

I swallowed hard to prevent a sound from escaping at referring to their, um, mature male companions as *boys*.

"—to keep them out of trouble and keep them out of the casino. At least keep them from going without us."

Three tittered appreciation for the leader's witticism. Coral complained, "I can't go to the pool. I can't get this cast wet."

She shrugged. "We'll be back later for a steam."

"Did you hear what I said? I can't get the cast wet. I can't go in the steam room."

"Oh. See you later."

"Tell Fabe that I—"

They'd gone. She remained.

After hearing two deep sighs, I slowly lowered the magazine I wasn't reading.

Coral was staring—not at the oceanic panorama from the wall of windows, but at her nails.

"Hi," I said brightly. Hey, go with the classics, right? "That's quite the cast." Skipping the fall seemed a good strategy. I'd bet she'd heard questions and comments about that from nearly everyone. "You're the passenger who had to go to the hospital in Gibraltar, aren't you? That must have been dramatic."

She looked up. Intrigued?

"And scary," I added.

"Terrifying," she said with great emphasis. "To be alone and in such awful pain, surrounded by foreigners. I couldn't understand a thing they said."

Alone? Her husband went with her and they'd had cruise line liaisons. As for those foreigners, Gibraltar was held by the British. For Coral, maybe the Queen's English was a foreign language.

Nope. Wasn't saying any of that.

"How awful. It's a miracle you rejoined the cruise."

"I wasn't letting them go on without me." From that strident statement, she went limp. "No matter what it cost me."

Them. Her friends? Or did she mean something else?

"It's understandable you don't want to miss out when you have a group that's been traveling together for a long time."

"For years and years. Might even be five by now. Except some," she ended darkly.

"Oh?" I hoped that would start her talking. Instead, she humphed. *Use your words, Coral.* Remembering what Coral shouted at Piper before pushing her onto the windows, I added, "Sometimes someone new coming into a group changes the dynamic. Changes how everyone interacts."

"*That's* the truth. I mean, Fabe—Faber—has known Boyd forever and he fits in with the boys. Even though when they play golf and need a *four*some, he makes five. But Fabe says a lot of times one of them can't play or they want to invite business associates and they can do two foursomes or something like that. And he's been good for their, like, networking, you know. New blood."

"You don't play golf?"

"God, no. None of us do. Except Piper. And isn't that just wonderful when they ask her to fill a second foursome or something. Her and the boys." Her sarcasm knew no subtlety. "She gets along great with them."

"And with the girls...?" I lightly prodded.

"She acts like she's been with us all along or is the most important or something. If I came into a new group I'd be, like, letting the others go first, you know? Humble."

"At least she was there for you when you fell."

"Fat lot of good she did. She stood there, staring."

"How *did* you fall, by the way?"

"What do you mean how did I fall? I went backward."

"Why? You said it wasn't your shoes. What was it?"

She huffed impatiently. "It was the damn stairs. I don't care how many times they say there was nothing wrong and they can show us all the pictures in the world. There was something there, under my foot. Something round and hard. It rolled when I stepped on it. And I went backward. Fabe'll sue their asses."

My murmuring of how awful that was opened the way for her monologue about her injuries and treatment, while I thought about other things.

Why would Leah trip Coral with her cane, then wait to threaten her until the night before Leah died. Leah could have thought she'd dealt with whatever problem Coral posed her with the fall.

But Leah's comments to the person by the elevator sounded more like Leah was the threat to that person. Not the other way around.

So, why had she tripped Coral?

She drew a breath. I jumped in. "Do you or your friends know any of the people onboard this cruise?"

She looked at me like I was an idiot. "Of course, we do. We know each other at home, like I said."

As gently as I could, I said, "Besides your group. Do any of you know anyone outside your group?"

She jerked an uninterested shoulder. "Nah."

"But you've been on this cruise before, right? Some of the same crew and staff and officers have been on the ship."

"Oh, *them*. I thought you meant like real *people*."

If metaphorical tongue-biting drew blood I would have been covered in it. "Do you know any of them?"

"Nah."

If she wasn't bored by the topic, she was a great actress.

❖   ❖   ❖   ❖

"HELLO, DEAR, FOUND your earring?" the elderly man asked as I came down the stairs from the spa deck.

Earring? Oh. Right. That's why he looked familiar. He'd been one of the searchers. I need an app to keep track of my fibs.

"I did. Thank you for your help and thank you for asking."

"Very nice."

He leaned in close for a look. But since I wasn't wearing earrings I couldn't imagine what he hoped to see. Then he stumbled, as if the ship had rocked. There'd been increasing movement interspersed with spells of calm. That had been a calm stretch.

He pretended to try to right himself by grabbing for me. Specifically, grabbing for the girls.

I'd been a public figure for a decade and a half. There's a certain segment of the population who takes that literally, treating my figure as if it were public property.

As I dodged out of his path, someone came in from my left, interposing itself between us.

"Sir. How dare you," scolded Petronella, more decisive than I'd ever heard her. "Shame on you."

She grasped my elbow and, before the elderly man or I could react, she marched me out of grabbing distance.

I released my elbow, but continued beside her.

"I appreciate your motives, Petronella, though you do know I can take care of myself, don't you?"

"If you could, you'd be in your cabin, resting. You look tired." Petronella could sting after all. Maybe not a wasp, but edging toward a sweat bee.

"I don't feel tired."

"You look *exhausted*." Ouch. She'd amped it up to honey bee. "You'll rest in your cabin and I'll stay there to be sure no one disturbs you."

"I can't rest with anyone else there. That's why I have to have my own cabin," I ad-libbed.

"Oh." The newly decisive Petronella deflated. "Well, I'm taking you to your cabin." She rallied to add, "And unplugging your phone."

CHAPTER THIRTY-FOUR

MY POOR LONELY balcony had company for a while that afternoon, thanks to Petronella.

True to her word, she unplugged the cabin phone, which had not rung once during this cruise that I was aware of. I pledged to rest and she finally left, saying she was going to her cabin, but she would be on guard that no one bothered me.

I could have resisted.

I could have slipped out as soon as she left me.

Truth be told, I felt the need of quiet to sort through what I knew, and what I didn't.

With a cruise liner pad of paper and pen I sat at the small balcony table, making notes. The ocean hadn't calmed and the clouds remained. But no rain fell and my cabin was high enough to miss any spray. The sea air and sounds of the ocean clapping against the ship proved as restorative as a nap.

My cell phone chimed with an arriving text.

Aunt Kit.

Her voice sounded in my head as I read it:

What are you being told, by whom, and why?

Odette flashed into my mind. A lot of my background information came from her, especially about the Marry-Go-Rounders. That was the *whom* and *what*. *Why* remained.

It didn't occur to me until now, with you asking these questions.

Was that true? Or had Odette led me to the brink of those questions? Had she molded my thinking about the Marry-Go-Rounders?

To believe she was so open and honest about what had happened and how she felt about it that I couldn't possibly suspect her.

Even before there was a murder.

Which would mean....

I shuddered. Could I be so wrong about a person?

Yes.

She certainly hid things—don't we all? She could have any number of secrets. Including, possibly, that the rub between her and Leah wasn't solely competition? That she wanted revenge against Leah for stealing Wardham? That she still loved him? In fact, she'd had no reason to confide in me what she had confided.

Was that confiding, by itself, suspicious?

I needed to talk to Odette.

Then I remembered my first thought on finding Leah, *Did Maya finally crack?*

I needed to talk to Maya, too, if I could get past Ralph.

Maybe asking Maya about Leah's troll reviewer role would open that door.

I didn't necessarily see Leah's Dee North persona as a motive for murder. If Aunt Kit had been aboard, maybe, considering her view on those who treated reviewing as a blood sport.

As it was, it would have made more sense for Leah to kill Maya for giving away her secret.

How could I—?

A second text came in. This time from Imka.

Constantine would end his shift at the poolside bar in half an hour.

❖   ❖   ❖   ❖

I CALLED ROOM service and had three chocolate desserts delivered anonymously to Petronella's cabin.

I was poised when the waiter arrived with them. From a crack in my door, I watched her answer and follow the waiter back inside with the tray. That's when I bolted out of my cabin and down the hallway the other direction.

The elevator doors opened almost immediately. I was a bit out of breath when I said, "Hi," brightly to the redheaded Valkyrie, alone in the elevator.

Her "Hi" conveyed considerably less enthusiasm.

"I'm glad I ran into you." That at least got her to look at me. "Is Coral really hurt? Or is the cast for show?"

Elevators don't leave time for subtlety.

"Why should I tell you anything?"

I debated with myself for less time than it took her to turn away. "Because of our mutual friend, Jason."

She stopped turning and looked at me. "You're friends with Jason?"

"Not the way you are. Our bond is over champagne and tips. Yours is much more ... personal. The kind of bond a husband might be interested in—"

She stopped my first attempt at blackmail with a vulgar and vehement word.

I interpreted that as a change of heart about my questions. "Is Coral's injury real?"

"How the hell would I know? I'm not her nurse."

"Have you seen anything that made you speculate or wonder if she isn't as badly injured as she's said?"

"I don't have to speculate. She makes a big deal over a scratch. So, yeah, she's not hurt as bad as she's crying about."

"What about the cast? Is that real?" She stared. I kept on. "Could she possibly take it off?"

"Take it off? It's not like a bracelet or something, you know."

I did know. Darn it.

It would be so much easier if she wore a walking cast that could come off in a pinch. A brace would be even better. But she had an old-fashioned cast.

I wasn't ready to give up, though.

The ding announced we'd reached the top deck.

"If you have any reason to think she could take that cast off, text me immediately." I wrote my number on the pamphlet with the day's activities stacked in a holder.

She took it, but as the doors opened, she growled, "Right."

"Give my regards to your husband."

She sent back a gimlet glare. I smiled.

CHAPTER THIRTY-FIVE

AT THE POOLSIDE bar I ordered a Virgin Mary from Constantine and tipped him generously.

He noticed. Enough to remember me.

He was the young bartender who'd had scotch splashed on him by Mr. Grandpa's Sailboat on the Label.

I didn't want to hang at the bar. I drank up, then retired around the corner to the soft ice cream machine. From there I could see Constantine. Ice cream after all that tomato juice was a bit strange, but I could live with it.

His replacement arrived and I followed Constantine from the bar to the storage closet with the tunics.

When he came out, he spotted me immediately. He also looked concerned immediately.

Poor kid. Had he been stalked before? But my intentions were entirely pure. I wanted his mind, not his body.

"Imka said you could help me with information to find out what happened, to help, uh, anyone who's innocent." I didn't want to mention names or murder in public.

"I can't talk to you, ma'am. If I'm seen—"

I retreated toward a corner. He hesitated. I dumped the contents of my bag on the deck.

He took an automatic step toward me—or toward the mess, because he was that well trained—then his mouth rounded slightly in an *oh* of comprehension.

"Let me help you, ma'am." He had a slight accent, but showed complete comfort with English.

"Thank you. Constantine?" Checking in case his nametag wasn't right.

He nodded.

We both scooched down.

"Imka told me to talk to you." I spoke fast and low. "She says you're friends with Badar."

"We're roommates and hang around together."

A distinction, which might make him less likely to fudge the truth and therefor more valuable.

"Did you see him the night before last?"

"Yeah. We were in our cabin. We played, uh, a computer game."

He was lying about something. But did the hesitations mean consumption of alcohol or illicit substances? Something else? Or that Badar had no alibi.

"How late?"

"Late, but I don't remember exactly. We weren't watching the clock."

I reached for a mini-packet of tissues that hadn't gone far, then asked on impulse. "Who else was there?"

"How'd you—? Nobody."

My heart rose for Badar—an alibi. My heart sank for Imka—was his alibi another woman?

"Too late, Constantine."

He looked around again. "It's nothing. Playing music—computer games. That's all."

Then why try to cover the mention of music? And why did the word *music* tickle the hairs at the back of my neck.

I followed the tickle.

"Anya?" There were a lot more musicians on board, but that's came to mind.

His eyes widened. "No."

"Pyorte?"

"I'm not—"

You already did, Constantine. As long as he was flustered... "Did

Badar ever talk to you about the passenger who was killed, Leah Treusault? I mean before she was killed?"

He was relieved to move away from Pyorte. "Just that she was a b—That she wasn't nice. We all knew that. Same way on a cruise a year ago. She nosed around, asking about other guests, even sneaking into the crew area. But that's no reason for him or anybody to do that to her. If we killed people anytime one wasn't nice…"

"There'd be few passengers left," I filled in.

"Or enough crew to run the ship."

I opened my bag for him to drop in a towel clamp and container of sunscreen. "They had trouble on last year's cruise? She and her husband?"

"*She* had trouble with everyone last year. At least this year she was occupied with other guests. Mostly occupied. A year ago, she was yelling at every crew member, except—" He veered away from discussing who Leah didn't yell at—presumably the steward she'd harassed—but his face reddened. "Badar gave her back some of her own, and that made it worse."

"Could she have gotten him fired?"

He leaned away, retrieving a tube of lip gel. "Probably not. Another guest maybe could. But she's known by everybody. Top officers, too."

"You said she yelled at every crew member *except*. Except who?" On last year's cruise it probably would have been the young steward Imka told me about. This cruise, Pyorte.

He looked hunted. He rubbed his thumb over the tips of his fingers on his left hand. The fingertips were reddened with two showing skin flaking away from blistered areas.

My mouth opened, making a record-setting standing broad jump from Leah not yelling at Pyorte to a new conclusion long before the rest of me caught up.

"Pyorte is the one Leah Treusault never yelled at. And he's teaching you guitar."

"Me? How—I never said…"

"It's true, though, isn't it? And from the state of your fingertips, you've been practicing recently. I'm sure crew members who have cabins near yours will confirm you have been. So, *have* you?"

His head dropped, severing eye contact. *Fib alert!* "Yeah, we played that night. More Pyorte than me, because my fingers hurt. And because he's so good. We played, Badar played video games. There's nothing wrong about that."

I watched him listlessly pick up my spare sunglasses and place them in my bag.

"The guitarist Pyorte was with you the night the passenger named Leah died?"

Why on earth try to keep that a secret? But I bet Badar hadn't shared this with Edgars, or the Security Chief would be looking at a wider field. And Badar had told Imka his honor prevented him from saying what he was doing that night.

Huh?

"We weren't doing anything wrong," Constantine said. "No matter what—"

Uh-huh. His defensiveness said otherwise. But my money was on a rules infraction. Though, I supposed all three could be involved in killing Leah. Or one of them and the other two protecting him? Or Badar and Pyorte involved in the killing with Constantine covering?

But Badar told Imka it wasn't his secret... If he'd told her the truth.

"—the snitch next door is always saying. He wants absolute silence all the time."

I needed a moment to regroup. "Constantine, you could get in a huge amount of trouble. If your friends did something and you're providing a false alibi..." I shook my head. "So think carefully before you answer this: Are you saying you, Badar, and Pyorte were together all night?"

"Yeah." He answered right away. "But I crashed. They were still going—Pyorte's used to staying up late and Badar was wound up."

With Constantine asleep, it wasn't the best alibi for those middle-of-the-night hours, but it was better than they'd had before.

The comment about the occupant of the cabin next to his wanting absolute quiet reminded me of something…

Had it. Jason at the Wayfarer Bar the night I'd listened to Anya and Pyorte there, griping about Pyorte showing displeasure at Jason talking over the music.

"Do you know Jason, the bartender in the Wayfarer?"

Whoa.

I had not expected *that*.

Not that Constantine exploded or grimaced or anything overt. His micro-expression, though, told me more than he'd ever intended.

His reaction to Jason was revulsion.

Revulsion is strong stuff.

I certainly hadn't had that reaction to the champagne-pouring bartender.

Although, had he actually been generous? Or had he used the ship's resources in the form of good champagne to ingratiate himself to me?

That scuffed up any gloss on Jason.

All that passed through my head before I added quickly enough that it seemed natural.

"How do he and Pyorte get along?"

"I don't know."

"Do you hang out with him?"

"No. He doesn't mingle with the likes of Badar and me."

I gambled. "I suppose not, because he likes mingling with passengers, doesn't he? Especially young, female passen—Wait a minute."

His reaction already confirmed my guess.

"I think that's everything, ma'am." He accompanied that statement in a loud voice by dropping my half-empty water bottle into my bag. Then, quieter. "I already said too much. I can't tell you more."

"Thank you for your help."

We stood, me with my disorganized bag hooked over my shoulder.

He walked away.

I went the other direction.

Presumably looking thoughtful.

That's sure how I felt. He'd given me lots to think about.

Including the fact that to whatever extent this alibi covered Pyorte and Badar, it left Anya and possibly Imka unalibied.

In the meantime, before Badar was carted off, I needed to soften the spotlight on him, considering I'd focused it there.

As long as I was still in the neighborhood, I swung back by the soft ice cream machine.

Hey, it had been a tough day. I deserved a second cone.

Low clouds filtered the sunlight, but passengers filled most of the deck chairs around the nearby outdoor pool, relaxing. I waved to three people I'd met on excursions, but didn't see any of the Marry-Go-Rounders or anyone else I connected with Leah.

I made sure to wipe any vestiges of ice cream from my mouth before my next stop.

✧ ✧ ✧ ✧

GERARD EDGARS CAME out of a room next door to his office.

It had taken less effort to get through to him this time, but his reception wasn't as welcoming.

"This way, Ms. Mackey." He stood aside, his bulk in front of an open doorway, his extended arm directing me down the hallway.

It was courteous. It also was meant to divert me from the fact they were playing video in the room he'd come out of.

When the door opened, I'd heard conversation about adjusting contrast levels and using a degraining filter. Looking in as I passed the door, I saw a slice of a monitor showing a dark scene of lined-up deck chairs.

Once again, Edgars directed me to the solitary guest chair in his office, while Henri leaned against the wall.

"You said to come back if anything else occurred to me. And it has. It's the question of how badly injured is Coral, the woman who fell down the stairs and was treated at Gibraltar."

CHAPTER THIRTY-SIX

I DIDN'T GET an answer, but the question might have helped anyway.

"You see a connection between these two events?" he asked.

"Has to be considered, don't you think?"

"I am curious why you might think it."

I didn't answer directly. "Do you know Coral insists something tripped her on those stairs? She says it felt as if she stepped on something rounded and hard, which caused her foot to go out from underneath her, pitching her backward."

A flicker in the gaze pinned on me. "She said this to you?"

"Yes. But that doesn't mean a lot. From what I can tell, she's said it to anybody who'll listen and those who'd rather not. She must have said it to you or your staff."

"As it happens, she did."

"But you dismissed it as a vain, silly woman who didn't want to admit she'd tripped on her own vain, silly shoes."

Impassive silence.

I got it. He wouldn't acknowledge that about a passenger to a passenger.

"One thing Coral knows is shoes. She says she's been walking in heels since she was a baby. That doesn't mean she couldn't fall over on those upside-down Eiffel Tower structures, but it might mean it's worth listening to what she said about a specific aspect of her fall."

This time I followed up with impassive silence.

Another flicker—amusement, maybe?—then he asked, "A specific aspect of her fall?"

"That it felt as if she stepped on something round and solid that rolled under her foot."

"That conveys significance to you?"

"Leah's cane fits Coral's description and what I saw the day we boarded." I described Leah stopping on the stairs after the muster drill, raising her cane, staring at the configuration that would allow her to slide the cane onto a step in the next half-flight up, causing anyone stepping on it to almost certainly fall.

"Why would Mrs. Treusault do such a thing?"

"I don't know. But Coral probably does. If she'll tell us—You. You need to question her. Also, this has to raise enough questions in your mind to change your plans."

"In what regard?"

"You have a morgue. You can take the body to Tampa and turn the case and all the suspects over to U.S. officials. There are too many possibilities to hand over Badar as the only suspect to authorities in the Bahamas."

Chief Security Officer Edgars' gaze flickered again.

Did it mean he didn't want to turn the case over? He preferred to deal with authorities in Tampa?

"We will confer with officials in the next port the Diversion is berthed at."

The flicker had fooled me into momentary hope that I had more time. So much for that.

"And turn over your prime suspect?" I accused. "I don't think he did it. I think you're wrong. But if you turn Badar over to the officials tomorrow morning without them having access to all the other people involved, without any way of knowing the interactions on board, the connections and rivalries and histories, they can't have a fair investigation. All the other possible suspects will sail off and they won't have anybody but Badar to blame. That's not right."

"What proof do you have that Badar did not kill her?"

"What proof do you have that he did?" I shot back. "When I gave you the hint about him, I didn't think you'd latch onto the first suspect and not look any further."

He sat back. "Ms. Mackey, when you told us of the animosity between Mrs. Treusault and a crew member at the towel stand, we were already aware of the incident. We had reviewed the video and spoken with the crew member shortly after it."

"Good grief. You review all the video every day?"

"A passenger acting threateningly toward a crew member is notable," he said dryly. "As it happens, the crew member reported the incident to his supervisor."

I jumped on that. "See? Would someone do that if they intended to kill her?"

"He might not have intended such a thing, but was caught in a moment of anger. We have motive from her threats to have him dismissed, opportunity from his failure to produce an alibi, means. We did not, as you describe it, latch onto the first suspect, especially not based solely on your words. Now, if you—"

"Means? The cane, right? Have you found Leah's cane?"

I felt more than saw Henri start. I was keeping my focus on Gerard Edgars.

"I would ask why you would be interested in the victim's cane?"

"It fits what the doctor said about how she was killed, something held across her throat. She had it with her every time I saw her, but it wasn't by her body. If you found it in her cabin you'd have said so by now. So you don't have the cane—"

"How—" came from behind me.

Without looking away from me, the security chief raised his index finger from where it rested on his opposite arm and Henri subsided.

"Where is it?" I persisted.

"An interesting question. We do not know. Beyond that, we will not discuss such specifics with you, Ms. Mackey."

"Fine. Don't. But it sure sounds to me like a whole lot of other people have means, motive, and opportunity. As strong as his."

"You are free, of course, to write a letter stating such. We, however, shall be turning him over to the authorities at the first place we dock."

"But that's—"

A puff of subdued cheering came from next door.

Before we could do more than exchange looks, a knock on the door. At Edgars' invitation, a young officer poked his head in.

"We have cleaned up that footage, sir."

Gerard Edgars strode out. The young officer pivoted smartly and followed. Henri, too.

I considered staying put.

Just kidding.

In the absence of direct orders otherwise—and, let's be honest, possibly in the presence of direct orders otherwise—I was behind them in a flash. Unobtrusively, quietly, but there nonetheless.

It only required three strides to reach the other room. Edgars swung the door open, not bothering to close it behind him with Henri right at his hip. The message bringer also left it open, perhaps too well trained in not slamming doors in a passenger's face to break the habit. I didn't bother, either. I stayed close, figuring that would make me look like part of the team.

It worked.

As we entered, I saw rows of monitors, showing all sorts of angles of spots all over the ship, with a bigger screen in the middle. Unfortunately, broad backs blocked out the bigger screen from my view.

"This is it, sir."

I saw nothing but the back of jackets.

Then one of the men seated in front of monitors to the right saw the door swinging open from the movement of the ship and stood to close it. I slid partially into his space and had an angle on the big monitor.

In time to see a shadow disappear out of the shot, which was recognizable as the line of deck chairs where Leah's body had been.

I bit my lip to keep from demanding it be replayed.

My self-restraint was rewarded when Edgars said, "Repeat."

Rewind went by too fast to make sense of what I was seeing, but then it stopped and moved forward again at normal pace.

The shadow was a human form. Carrying something the size and shape of a Leah-like body wrapped in towels.

The shadowy human moved into deeper darkness, then emerged.

It wore a waiter's tunic, tennis shoes, and plain, dark, loose pants. The lack of light prevented me from identifying the few objects the figure passed, much less using them as a gauge of height.

"Again," Edgars said.

This time I concentrated on the way the figure moved at the beginning. It was a strange movement, awkward, as if the person were trying to avoid stepping in something, but nothing was visible on the deck.

It must be that carrying the bundle—presumably Leah—altered the figure's walk. Which meant it wouldn't help with identification.

I switched to concentrating on the deck chair. That was something tangible I could use as a gauge to "measure" the figure.

Except the shadows and loose pants made it hard to tell where on the carry-er's leg the deck chair came.

I squinted harder at the image. If this was the cleaned-up version, the original must have been a mess.

But as they played it a third time, I became more confident. The person was about my height of five-eight, with an inch or two leeway, either side.

If the leeway stretched to three inches, Wardham and Ralph remained in the suspect pool. All the women fell in that range, including the ill-tempered German woman, though she was on the short end of possible.

"Ms. Mackey." Gerard Edgars faced me with his impressive arms crossed over his chest.

Oops. I'd been spotted.

✧　✧　✧　✧

AFTER I WAS escorted to the passenger area, I saw I'd received a text.

The shops and main desk were crowded because rain and wind drove everyone inside. Took me a while to find a spot without a dozen people looking over my shoulder to read the text.

They take him TOMORROW!!! You must DO something!!!! Now!!!!!

Imka had gone for subtle.

CHAPTER THIRTY-SEVEN

THE DINING ROOM was almost empty at dinner. Our waiter was absent, replaced by the head waiter.

I didn't notice until halfway through the meal and asked the others where everybody was.

"Sheila comes up from the depths of thinking serious thoughts," Bob said.

"Don't be teasing the girl, Robert," Catherine admonished. "She's trying to solve a murder."

Petronella gasped. "Oh, no. You're not involved in that horrible thing, are you? I mean I know you found poor Leah, but to get as far away as possible from what happened must be your only wish."

Catherine made a sound I couldn't spell. It told Petronella not to be silly using only consonants. "But of course she is. They're taking that boy off this ship tomorrow and giving him to the officials in the Bahamas as the only suspect. Unless Sheila can unravel the mess."

Gee, thanks for the pressure, Catherine.

Petronella's eyes widened to goggling.

"That boy's being blamed when it's pure bigotry," Catherine added.

Petronella blinked. "Bigotry? His race? Nationality?"

"His mood," I said. "I think Catherine's saying they're prejudiced against him because he can be surly."

Bob laughed and Petronella relaxed.

"As for your question, Sheila," Bob said, "the rough seas have brought on an epidemic of seasickness. Even laid low our waiter, who, as she told us numerous times, has worked many cruises. We're one of the few hardy tables intact."

I suppose the ship was moving more than usual, but it wasn't *that* bad.

Though I was grateful for the abundance of railings when we left the dining room. Bob and Catherine headed for another show—"We'll get the prime seats with the field thinned by this," Bob crowed—while I declared my intention to go to my cabin.

To think.

Might as well have said to fret.

A lurch sent me grabbing for a railing as a couple stumbled out of the Wayfarer Bar. No way to know who was drunk and who wasn't, thanks to the ship's rolling.

Petronella started to come with me to the corridor where our cabins were, then abruptly stopped and said she'd forgotten something.

✧ ✧ ✧ ✧

MY SHEETS OF paper covered the bed. I'd stared at them to no purpose for a good hour, when a knock sounded at my door.

I felt as if I'd spent every minute since finding Leah's body running around asking questions. The answers remained a jumble.

Getting up disturbed a few of the pages, but no harm done, since nothing made sense anyway. Then a roll of the ship nearly took me off my feet.

Another knock. Not very patient.

Before I stumbled my way around the bed, more banging rattled the door and Petronella called, "Sheila, Sheila, I have something to tell you."

I made it to the door by pressing my hands to the walls on either side of the narrow entry for balance.

"What's the matter? You're not seasick, are you?"

"No, thank heavens." She clearly wasn't. Just as clearly she had far better sea legs than I did.

If the ship rocked and rolled like this the first day, many more than Coral would have fallen, with or without a cane being stuck under their feet.

I stumbled my way back, past the bed, to the sofa. She followed me with no problem, staring at the bedspread of notes as she came past.

"What are you doing?"

"Trying to organize ideas about suspects, motives, timing."

"Oh, dear. All these are suspects?"

"A lot of them are. Because any one of them could have done it."

"Oh, no." Petronella clasped raised hands to her chest.

"You do realize it has to be someone on the ship?"

That startled her. After a pause, she said, "I suppose." Though she appeared to be longing for the possibility of a murderous ultra-marathon swimmer. "But surely someone we haven't met?"

"That's possible."

She brightened.

"Not probable."

Her face fell. "But why?"

"Murder is most often committed by a person who knows the victim. Stranger murder is relatively rare. One of the things I learned at Aunt Kit's knee over the past fifteen years."

She looked puzzled.

"You know Aunt Kit writes mysteries, don't you?" I asked her.

"Oh, yes. And other little books. Nothing important, like what you wrote, though."

I felt myself bristling in Kit's defense. Or in defense of all those "little" books. I'd heard it often enough from the publishing establishment.

Even though, in this case, having "my" book held up as superior to Kit's was sort of complimenting her ... while insulting her.

"Have you read any of Kit's mysteries?"

"Oh, no, I couldn't. Tony doesn't approve."

Tony was a beer-swilling beer-gutted bully. Why on earth he'd object to her reading mysteries was beyond me.

"Now you're divorced from Tony, you can," I said cheerfully.

Her eyes filled with tears.

Before she slid irretrievably into lachrymose, I said, "Aunt Kit's are excellent, and she does lots of research to get things right. I've listened to her tell me about the research and joined her in some of it. We've toured police stations and talked to the FBI and ATF and lots of other people to find out about murders."

"Oh, dear. Murders?"

"Of course."

"But she writes mysteries."

CHAPTER THIRTY-EIGHT

MY FIRST RESPONSE was a blank, *Huh?* "You do know mysteries are almost always about a murder, don't you?"

Her eyes widened. "Kit's written about murder? How awful."

I slid past that point for the moment.

"I'm glad she has, because Aunt Kit's research and what she's taught me about murders and investigating is all I have to work with now."

"Why?"

"Because there's been a murder on board," I reminded her.

"But why you? Shouldn't you let the officials handle this?"

Why me? Because I'd have to answer to Kit if I didn't get involved. Or if I didn't *stay* involved. To the end.

In fact, I'd answer to Kit *and* to Imka.

I responded to the other part of Petronella's question. "They appear to be stymied." Also locked myopically on Badar. "More important, they don't know the people like I—" I had an idea. "—like we do. We know their backgrounds and personalities. At least some."

"But it could be anyone."

"I don't think so. Most murders are committed by someone who knows the victim. On this ship, that's a limited number of people. And we know them. Let's consider them one by one."

She stared at me.

"This'll be good." Maybe sorting thoughts aloud would work better than rearranging pages. Couldn't be worse. "We'll start with the most likely suspect. Wardham."

She gasped. "That sweet man?"

I had my doubts, too. Not based on sweetness, but apparent weakness. A pose? Protective covering against a wife like Leah? But then how would a strong man end up married to a woman like her. On the other hand, why would Odette have ever married a man as ineffectual as Wardham appeared to be? Could he have changed drastically during his marriage to Leah?

Then, at the extreme edge of *maybe* was the idea of someone killing Leah to break Wardham's heart. It would have taken a remarkably unobservant murderer not to have noticed how she treated him.

The paper listing that theory had fallen off the bed when I stood and I'd kicked it under the bed on my way to the door.

"No matter how seemingly sweet, the spouse is always a prime initial suspect according to Aunt Kit. Has to be looked at for sure. In this case, everybody had means. They could hold her cane across her throat and, since she was so small, they—" I caught Petronella's expression and stopped. "Right. No details. He had means. Also opportunity. He said he was in the cabin sleeping, but there's no proof, so it's wide open. And motive—well, that's obvious."

"What motive could he possibly have? Why would he ever kill his *wife*?" she asked. "No, no, I can't believe it of him."

I suspected her unwillingness to consider any husband would consider killing any wife was projection. Or denial. Heck, I'd heard her apply the same denial to divorce, despite Tony already finalizing theirs.

"Look at their marriage, Petronella. She wasn't at all nice to him. She bossed him around and did nothing for him."

Remind you of any other marriages, Petronella? Tony told everyone— including within Petronella's hearing—their irreconcilable difference was "She's boring as sh—"

She froze like a bunny in the middle of the lawn with our big, goofy childhood golden retriever, Bounce, bounding toward it.

"Some people like caring for those they love," she said in a small voice.

"And that's wonderful. But when the other party doesn't acknowledge, appreciate, or reciprocate the generosity, it has to be wearing." Without looking at her, I lightly added, "It could make someone like Wardham into a doormat. If he became tired of being a doormat no one could blame him, but—"

"But *murder*."

Did Petronella recognize her doormatness? Had she ever considered ways to change it?

"If he wasn't strong enough to stand up to her, to get out of the marriage—can you imagine what Leah would say and how she'd make him suffer—he might have seen it as his only solution. Plus, he had another motive." I slid a look toward her. "Odette."

"Odette? But…"

"You saw him coming out of her cabin. She might, unwittingly, have sparked him to act."

As I said it, though, I wondered about *unwittingly*. I didn't see Odette as unwitting about any situation.

Petronella shook her head. "I can't believe it of him."

"Then how about Ralph?"

"What? That handsome man?"

Handsome is as handsome does shot to my lips. I clamped them closed.

"His motive could be anger at the way Leah threw him over. Or it could be anger—or protectiveness—over Leah's treatment of Maya."

I read in her face that she rather liked the idea Ralph might have battled the dragon for lady fair. What she said was, "But Maya said he was with her in the cabin all night. They both said that."

News to me. "When did they say that?"

"Yesterday. Right before we found you looking for your earring." With some triumph, she added, "That gives him an alibi."

I waved that away. "Lying to protect him. Or to protect herself. Because Maya might have done it, too. In which case Ralph was lying about being in the room together to protect her. Sometimes a mutual alibi doesn't alibi either party." Kit used that plot point recently.

Petronella frowned at me as she puzzled out what I'd said. "I don't understand."

I refused to feel a twinge of fellowship with Tony. "If one person lies about being with the second person and the second person agrees, both people are unaccounted for at the important time."

"Oh... *Oh*, yes, I see. But do you think Maya... I mean she might lie, but would she really *hit* someone? She's ... gentle."

Her tone didn't sound enchanted with the female version of Wardham as an uber sensitive soul.

"Even the gentle can get fed up. And Leah did a lot to make her fed up."

"Maya *did* marry *her* husband."

She gave that enough snap to make me wonder if she'd heard Tony was lining up a second Mrs. Domterni. "*Ex*-husband," I emphasized. "And Leah instigated the ex-ness."

Petronella pursed her lips and blew out a breath. It was almost a humph. Pretty wild for her.

"One question is if Maya could have carried Leah the way the figure in the security footage did."

"Yes."

The crisp, solitary word brought my head up. "Yes, that's a question or, yes, she could have carried her?"

"Maya could have carried Leah. That's what I came to tell you. Bob was impressed with your trying to solve this murder—" I could have sworn that was Catherine. "—and I thought maybe I was being old-fashioned, thinking I needed to keep you away from all that. So, when I saw Ralph and Maya in the Wayfarer Bar after dinner, I went in and chatted with them. They said they had cabin fever—

"Ha! Cabin fever on a ship."

"—and came out tonight because so few people were around. What?"

"Never mind. Go ahead."

"I'm afraid they don't want to talk with you. They say you're nosy. But we chatted and they said a few things."

"That's great, Petronella. What did they say?"

"You don't mind me talking to them even after they said you're too nosy?"

"I'm thrilled they talked to you. What did they say?"

"What they said tonight or...?"

"Anything relevant. Anytime."

"Did you know Maya was an athlete in college? A couple days before you, uh, found Leah, I was sitting with them while you were in the pool—you really should be careful about how much sun you get. Odette tried to get her to go with to the fitness center. Maya said there was too good a chance she'd see Leah, who'd gone for a steam. Odette said she shouldn't let Leah keep her from being as powerful and fit as she was in college. Then Maya said she could still do what she needed to, even if she was carrying extra weight. Then Ralph said he loved every bit of her and Odette said of course he did and Maya was beautiful and Maya cried. But Ralph teased her about carrying the dog and by the end he had her laughing."

She sighed. I suspected Petronella envied Maya the attentive and protective Ralph. Which raised the question of how far he'd go to protect his current wife from his ex-wife.

Keeping the focus on Maya, I asked, "What about her carrying a dog?"

"Maya said she picked up her dog and carried him to the car when he got hurt. A huge dog."

"Recently?"

"Since she and Ralph married, because he was talking about it, too."

She looked at me expectantly, waiting for me to make the connection. "So if she could carry a big dog, she could have carried Leah."

"I thought, maybe… But if I'm wrong—"

"You're not. Good job, Petronella."

Three people from that group, three possibilities. We hadn't yet discussed the final member. Odette.

As if she'd heard my thought, Petronella said, "There must be other people who might have done this horrible thing."

"Along with Badar, the guy they're zeroing in on, there are several nice, young crew members you like who have to be considered."

She looked uncertain, torn between passengers she knew and "nice young people" being a murderer.

"You mean like the boy who plays the guitar and the girl who plays the violin?"

"Yes, I do." I'd mentioned them to Edgars and Henri, but hadn't found out anything beyond Constantine giving Pyorte an alibi. Although that left Anya unaccounted for, not to mention being in the hallway near Leah's cabin the next morning. And in tears.

On the other hand, Leah was already dead and in the deck chair hours before I saw Anya in the corridor. No apparent blood on her. Definitely not in possession of Leah's cane. But could she have been trying to retrieve something incriminating from Leah's cabin? If so, the authorities hadn't found it.

Or.

They *had* and they hadn't mentioned it to me.

"What made you think of them?" I asked Petronella.

"The scene in the hallway."

I blinked. She'd seen Anya that morning and hadn't mentioned it? "Scene in the hallway?"

She looked confused for a moment. "Oh. You weren't there. It was when I went to the ladies' room after they played in the Atrium. The sloe gin fizz went right—"

"The scene?"

"The boy—young man, I suppose I should say, though where the line is these days—"

"The guitarist?"

"Right. Him. He was sort of in a corner, holding his guitar in front of him and Leah was right up against it, pressing it into him. I couldn't have been comfortable for him at all. Leah was talking a mile a minute, real low, so you couldn't hear the words, but the poor boy—young man—was red as a beet. Then the girl came with her violin. She put the bow right in front of Leah's face and Leah kind of screeched."

"Then what?"

"I went in the ladies' room." Reading my expression, she said, "I suppose you wish I'd seen how it ended? I'm sorry, Sheila. I'm really sorry. It's those sloe gin fizzes. They just go right through—"

"Okay. I know. You certainly added more information. That's very helpful."

"I, uh … Would other information about Leah be helpful? Would you want to hear if—?"

"Yes, I want to hear."

"It was a little thing. Nothing really."

Holding onto my patience, I repeated, "I want to hear."

"It was the day after Coral came back on board. I wanted to ask her if she was truly all right. But she was with her friends and Leah was there. I waited a bit to see if I'd have a chance without interrupting, but Leah said something about *now you see what I'm capable of* and *I haven't forgotten last year*. Coral was really angry and almost pushed her and said something about *crazy old lady*. Leah laughed and left, but after that, I could see Coral wasn't in a good mood and I didn't want to go up to them, so I never talked to her."

Now you see what I'm capable of.

I haven't forgotten last year.

Interesting. Didn't make sense … I added a mental and hopeful, *Not yet.*

It turned out Petronella had another sloe gin fizz with Maya and Ralph in the bar and couldn't possibly use the bathroom in my cabin.

I escorted her to the door to make sure she got to her cabin without being lurched off her feet.

"Good sleuthing, Petronella," I said as she walked out.

She flushed.

Her path didn't even waver. She must have been a sailor in a past life.

As I closed the door, I realized something else, and said a soft, "Good for you," under my breath.

In this whole conversation she hadn't once said, "Oh, no, I couldn't possibly."

CHAPTER THIRTY-NINE

WITH THE MOVEMENT of the ship, I slept and woke. Not sure when I dreamed, when I remembered, when I imagined.

Leah pointing her cane at the German woman.

Anya crying in the corridor.

The lyrics to *The Fields of Athenry*.

Maya, no longer teary, on the attack at the hot tub. Ralph, ever protective of her.

Coral pushing Piper into the windows and Imka's hold on Piper.

T-bar and errand chase sonar. You and me theme and Cheese Mary now.

Aunt Kit saying, *Stop making words. Say the sounds. Let go of the words and say the sounds over and over.*

Wardham coming out of Odette's room.

The Valkyries in formation sweeping into the spa.

The German woman sneering at Leah.

The vitriol of Leah's reviewer persona.

Pyorte's hunted expression.

The voices from the Atrium bar.

Leah, cane overhead, as if to strike Badar.

I woke with a start, thinking it was the middle of the night.

The clock said otherwise. I stumbled toward the curtains, opening them to milky light. The ocean didn't look as rough as last night. The ship felt calmer than during the night, too.

But no calm waters ahead for Badar.

He was out of time. When we arrived in the Bahamas in a few hours, he'd be turned over to the authorities as the only suspect.

❖   ❖   ❖   ❖

AFTER ROOM SERVICE breakfast, I was on my balcony, taking a break from looking—again—at the notes by watching the still active ocean when my cell phone rang. I hadn't heard the sound since we left Barcelona.

Aunt Kit.

"Your mother called me—"

"Mom? Why did she call you? Is everything okay?"

She snorted. "Everything's fine. She called me because she doesn't want you to pay roaming charges, even though I've told her more than once how much money you have."

"You don't care about roaming charges?"

"I wouldn't care about them under these circumstances even if you were a pauper. I certainly don't now. Besides, my motivation is stronger than your mother's. She is merely over the moon that you wrote to them about possibly moving back to their part of the country—" The internet must have connected at some point and sent my pending emails. "—while I want to hear everything about this murder and your investigation."

"*My* investigation? That's not—"

"No false modesty. Besides, better to be prepared. If word gets out the author of *Abandon All* solved a murder…"

I groaned.

"Never mind that now, tell me everything."

"First, I have to tell you it's too late."

"What do you mean it's too late?"

"We're stopping in the Bahamas today. The ship's Chief Security Officer will hand over a young crew member as the only suspect and I don't think they'll investigate anymore."

"Is this young crew member innocent?"

"Not necessarily. But there are several other people with as much evidence against them as there is against him. I'm afraid he's convenient."

"You sound disappointed."

"I am," I realized. "I think I expected better of Edgars, the Chief Security Officer."

"Hmm. Let's get back to telling me everything."

I did.

At the end, I added, "I've been trying to treat it the way we would in a session at the brownstone. Thinking my way logically through and—"

"What's bothering you?" she interrupted.

"You mean other than a woman being murdered and me finding the body and having a sweet young woman putting all her faith in my getting her boyfriend off when he's turned over to the authorities today?"

"Yes, other than that. There's something gnawing at you. What?"

Saying *nothing* was a waste of time. She was almost always right about these things.

"It doesn't make any sense—"

"Good. In fact, excellent. What is it?"

"Early on, I overhead some people talking from another deck and with the wind and me drifting asleep, the last part made no sense. Like nonsense syllables. But I can't get them out of my head. See, I told you it doesn't make sense."

"What are the syllables?"

"T-bar and errand chase sonar. You and me theme and cheese Mary now." My immediate recall surprised me. "But as I said, it's nonsense."

"The words you created from the sounds make no sense. Stop making words. Say the sounds. Let go of the words and say the sounds over and over. Then see—"

A crisp knock sounded at my door. Not Eristo's polite restraint.

"Someone's at the door, Kit."

"Okay. Call me when you can, never mind the roaming charges. And plan a good long talk about this after. Are you taking notes?"

More knocking.

"I haven't—I have to go, Kit." Before the knocker became even more insistent. "I'll call."

I fumbled to turn off my phone as I opened the door to Catherine.

CHAPTER FORTY

SHE MOVED PAST me, leaving me at the door. "Close it, close it. Did you hear?"

Since my answer to that question from her was always no because she heard things first, I said, "What?"

"We're not stopping in the Bahamas."

"What? Really?"

"The official reason is the weather's too windy—"

"But it's better."

"Because we sailed away from the rough weather overnight. We're well away from the Bahamas right now. Anyway, the official reason is it wasn't safe to use the tender to get us to the beach—"

"Oh, my God, the *tender*."

That sneaky, sneaky Edgars.

We, however, shall be turning him over to the authorities at the first place we dock.

He'd said that to make me think Badar would be dropped in the Bahamas as the culprit while they washed their hands of him and the investigation, the entire time knowing the Diversion wouldn't *dock* until Tampa.

"—but the rumor is it's even more because the Bahamas don't want this investigation. *Oh, my God, the tender* what?"

"I think you might be right. Or the cruise officials don't want to hand the investigation over to them." I told her what Edgars said. "But we were never going to *dock*. Because they use the tender to transport passengers to that beach. Why give me a song and dance about it?" I shook my head. "Never mind. If they're not taking Badar off, we have time—some time."

"Not *we*. *You*, Sheila."

"No, definitely we. Lots of we. You should have heard Petronella last night. She was helping me sort out the possible suspects, plus adding observations. And all the information you've brought?" I gestured for her to sit on the couch. "Let's think this through, starting with the basics. Means, motive—"

"How much time do you have? The list could cover everyone on the ship."

I acknowledged that with a grimace.

"—opportunity. Means is probably her own cane, which—"

"Now that's something I didn't know."

"I overheard the doctor after I found her. He said there was a skin tear—" I hadn't mentioned the blood on my finger to anyone beyond the ship officials. "—but it probably happened when someone did the same damage as strangling would, by putting something hard and round across her throat."

"Nasty."

"How much strength would that take?" I asked rhetorically. "She was small and not strong, but people don't die from strangling or this version of it in a few seconds. It had to be someone strong enough to control her. Plus, they haven't found her cane. Not anywhere."

"There's an argument, the murderer takes her cane away, and uses it against her?"

"Mmm-hmm. Then wraps her in towels and carries her to the chair. Presumably because they didn't want an examination of where the murder occurred. But why that spot? You know, that video took a lot of work to get it improved to the point it could be called awful. But other shots I saw running in the room were quite clear."

Her eyebrows went up. "Someone fooled with the video?"

"They wouldn't have to. That spot has lousy lighting. Especially at night. I think it was chosen for that reason. And, think about this, Catherine, if Edgars had clear video from anywhere else in the ship, like where she was killed or of the murderer carrying her, he'd use it to make an identification."

"Meaning nothing else shows on video?"

"Exactly. Which means the person knew where the security cameras covered and where they didn't."

"My, oh, my."

"So, who knows where the security cameras covers?"

"The head of security," she said immediately. I almost wished... She quickly went on, "Truly, I'd say most of the crew, if not all. They're human. Surely things go on they don't want known."

"Makes sense. And they'd learn and share with each other."

"They would. Repeat passengers, as well, learning and sharing. I've heard a frequent cruiser in his cups tell another how to get from one cabin to another without anyone the wiser. I couldn't repeat it now, but there are some who could trace the path."

She'd confirmed my speculations. Unfortunately, it didn't eliminate any of the possibilities listed on my notes. "I have another question for you, cruise expert that you are. Why would Badar and a bartender be nervous about people knowing the guitarist, Pyorte, was in their room?"

"A bartender? That numpty, Jason?"

"That—? Never mind. I can tell from your tone." Though I hate to think too badly of someone who served me Veuve Clicquot.

"It's not crude," she said in mock indignation.

"Too bad. What do you know about him?"

She hitched a shoulder. "That I'd swear an oath to?"

"Between us."

"He's known multiple female passengers in the biblical sense, no matter the rule against fraternizing between crew and guests. He pursues them. None worry about a budget."

I remembered his exchange of looks with the Valkyrie named Piper. Was something going on there as well as with the redhead? I wouldn't have said it was sexual. Or... not *only* sexual. There'd definitely been communication in it. But then there'd been his attention to the redhead.

Hold on to that for later.

"The bartender I meant wasn't Jason. It's a young guy. Nice. At the poolside bar."

"Constantine."

Of course she knew who I meant. "Yes. Why would he be worried? Him, Badar, and Pyorte. None were fraternizing with passengers." If anything, Pyorte did his darnedest not to fraternize with Leah.

"There are other rules they could be breaking."

Our gazes met.

She shrugged. "They have crew bars with drinks for considerably less than we pay, but some might want something else."

"Could be. But what other rules are possible?"

"Safety, health, politeness, no side jobs, though tips—"

"Side jobs?"

"They work for the cruise line. They're not to work another job."

I raised one "ah-hah" finger. "I wonder..."

Before I could voice my wondering, the PA system came to life.

The captain told us what I already knew thanks to Catherine—the Diversion wouldn't stop until we reached Tampa. Out of concern for the safety of the passengers.

The windy weather made use of the tender to reach the Bahama beach unsafe.

Catherine looked at me questioningly. I might have ground my teeth at the mention of the tender.

Was I making too much of myself to wonder if Edgars meant to turn the heat up on me like I was one of Odette's frogs?

Oh.

Frogs.

What if one of the frogs, *did* notice as it got hotter and hotter? What would it do? Especially if it had the means to strike down the person turning up the temperature?

Before exploring that, I had other important elements to pin down. Like my latest earworm.

✧　✧　✧　✧

I MADE A dash to the spa. Imka wasn't there. Under the disapproving frown of the receptionist, I asked her friend, Bennie, a handful of questions.

Then, I spent considerable time on my balcony, repeating the non-sense syllables—sounds—over and over. Hoping the wind would reorder them to somehow make sense.

No luck.

When my throat felt scratchy, I gave up.

That brain block remained.

But I'd had an idea about patterns.

PETRONELLA AND I ate lunch in the buffet, because she insisted I needed to get out of the cabin. Yesterday she'd wanted me in it, today out. Don't ask me.

She kept giving me concerned looks as we went from food station to food station.

"May we join you?"

Her question pulled me out of my fog and I realized she'd found the same marijuana-farm-bound young man at a table alone.

She looked at me like a cat who'd brought its first dead mouse home to its owners.

I maneuvered to put two table legs between us. He and Petronella carried the conversation. Turned out he liked to bake as much as she did. Though I suspected he added an ingredient to his brownies she didn't.

By the end of the meal, I'd made one decision, anyway.

When I stood, Petronella did, too. "I'm going with you."

"I'm going to talk to Odette, if she'll talk. I want to follow up on something, plus ask her about Wardham and—" I gave her a significant look. "—yesterday morning."

She swallowed hard. "I'm coming."

CHAPTER FORTY-ONE

I LED PETRONELLA to Odette's cabin, remembering the number Odette gave me more than a week ago, and knocked firmly.

Odette opened the door almost immediately. She didn't hesitate, inviting us in.

We sat on the couch, while she took the desk chair.

"Odette, did you know Leah was reviewing books under the name Dee North of Boise, Idaho?"

"No. I was as surprised as anybody when Maya brought it up. Though I can see Leah doing that. An online bridge discussion group we were on kicked her off because of her harsh posts. She rejoined under a new name and was kicked off again for the same thing. She wasn't shy about criticizing someone to their face, but the distance and anonymity of online forums..."

"You said you backed out of coming last year, but decided to give this year another try. Do you remember your specific thinking about those decisions?"

She raised her eyebrows in amusement and surprise. "My, quite a request. Let's see. A few days before the deadline to pay for the trip last year, after Ralph and Maya cancelled, I sat down and considered spending two weeks with Leah. Her sharpness had become increasingly mean around then. I decided I did not want to be exposed. And, indeed, she was particularly nasty before she and Wardham left on the cruise.

"She was so much better on their return that I felt, perhaps, I overreacted. And I did miss the cruising. As I've said, I persuaded Ralph and Maya to come again, too. I had second thoughts in the run-up to the trip because she was back to her old ways. But, after cancelling and regretting, I chose to stick it out."

"What about four years ago when Bruce Froster died and the couples re-coupled. Do you recall her behavior before that cruise?"

"It's a long time ago and with events during that cruise and after— No. Wait. I do recall some... Yes. Wardham and I had several talks about how razor sharp Leah's tongue had become. I remember, because it made his marrying her all the more ironic. What is this about, Sheila?"

"Would you be surprised to learn her reviews were particularly nasty during those three periods—before the cruise four years ago, before last year's cruise, and before this cruise? Followed by periods of relative normalcy."

Her quick mind got it immediately. "She built up frustration or whatever drove her, expiated it over the cruise, entering a calmer period, before—" She looked at me questioningly. "—the cycle began again?"

"Possible, don't you think?"

"Certainly possible."

"Then, the question is, what happened on last year's cruise to work off her built up frustration or whatever drove her. Did she mention anything about the cruise?"

"Mmm." She went silent, her gaze fixed. She blinked before she spoke. "She did say a few times that we'd really missed out, that last year was outside the usual cruise experience, that she'd discovered new entertainment, and was looking forward to more of it this year. No indication of what that entertainment was. I might have asked more as this trip neared, but she was back into her worst behavior."

"If you remember more..."

"Of course. If there's nothing else now—"

"There is."

I let the silence extend, feeling Petronella fidget beside me. Odette sat calmly.

"We saw you and Wardham yesterday morning."

"Did you?"

"Yes. And I will be telling the authorities what we saw."

"Is that what you came to tell me?"

"No. We came to ask you—"

"Why?" Petronella wailed.

Odette's brows rose as she smiled. "For sex."

That stopped Petronella.

"The night after his wife was found dead?"

"You know the answer, Sheila. Yes."

Petronella's head turned from me to Odette to me and ended facing Odette. "But… but you said you were better off without him. You said he hadn't aged well. You said you were having more fun without him. But—"

Uh-oh. Had Petronella seen Odette as a role model for getting over Tony? A role model who'd had ex sex. Would she take this as permission to pine for Tony?

"—you still *love* him," she finished.

"I did say those things. And each is true. However, I found myself wondering if there's still something to be said for an old-fashioned toaster."

"Toaster?" Petronella and I said together.

"Toaster. Instead of the fancy gadgets all the rage now, where you need a special course to be able to use. Instead, just slip the toast in the slot and be done with it. Wardham is the sexual version of an old-fashioned toaster. Oh, now I see I've shocked you…"

"You and Wardham are back together." Petronella's conclusion was an accusation.

"My personal life is personal," Odette said with an edge.

She'd acknowledge sex with her ex, but not talk about love.

Her earlier words explaining the relationships replayed in my head. What she'd said absorbed me then, but now the *how* of saying it.

Leah is married to my ex-husband, Wardham.

Leah and what she did, came first.

In relationship to Odette.

With the man himself almost an afterthought.

She is very competitive. Very. ... Not that I'm stronger, but that she considers she's beaten me.

Was Leah alone in seeing it as a game, in keeping score?

Could that kind of competition lead to—

Not there yet. Definitely not there yet.

Especially since I intended to ask the woman for a favor.

"Remember telling me about your friend who'd said she wouldn't have been surprised to hear Coral pushed Piper down the stairs, but was surprised by what did happen? Does that mean she has reason to think Piper pushed Coral down the stairs?"

"Oh. Interesting. I didn't think to ask. Do you want me to—?"

"If you could introduce us, I'd love to meet her in person."

Her mouth pursed. "No interference from me? No problem. I'll introduce you and leave. You can't ask for better. But it's a man, not a woman. And an acquaintance rather than a friend."

✧ ✧ ✧ ✧

"**VANCE, THIS IS** Sheila Mackey. She has questions you will answer nicely. Sheila, this is Vance Reesha."

It was Mr. Grandpa's Sailboat on the Label.

He leered. "What do I get in return?"

"Behave yourself, Vance," Odette said.

"You're no fun. But I suppose as long as I can't work on my tan on the upper deck—they've blocked off the whole section, say they don't know when or if it'll be reopened to passengers—I might as well."

Must be where he'd been when I overheard him.

I clamped my hand on Odette's arm. "Why don't you stay? You might be able to fill in gaps."

I could handle the lecher. But that would take time. And likely bruising. Certainly of his ego, possibly physical. Not conducive to getting answers from him. Odette could run interference without Mr. Grandpa's—Vance Reesha.

Besides, what I wanted from this guy had nothing to do with the

Marry-Go-Rounders, so she didn't have that big a conflict of interest.

A glint of humorous understanding came into her eyes. "Delight-ed."

Adopting Aunt Kit's most businesslike tone, I addressed him. "I understand you've crossed paths before with the members of a group of five couples sailing together."

He looked blank.

"Five wives, five husbands?"

More blank.

Odette cleared her throat. "Older men, flashily attractive younger women. One with a noteworthy, ah, derrière."

"Ohhhh. Yeah." I suppressed a squirm at his smile. "Let me tell you about them…"

As he did, I realized three things beyond what he was saying.

His was the voice I'd heard in the Atrium during the musicians' break, telling someone else about a man wanting to go back to his first wife.

His was also the voice I'd heard drifting into my drowsy brain that third day on the Diversion, when I'd heard a string of nonsense words.

T-bar and errand chase sonar you and me theme and Cheese Mary now?

That was the third and final thing I realized.

They weren't nonsense.

And I knew what he'd really said.

I wanted to confirm it without an audience.

"Odette, will you leave us alone, please."

"Now you're talking," he said with a leer.

CHAPTER FORTY-TWO

My conversation with Chief Security Officer Gerard Edgars started with, "I have a theory and an idea" and ended with "What have you got to lose?"

That might have been what persuaded him to agree—reluctantly—to bring together the list of people I requested in an empty suite.

"Hey," the Valkyrie leader objected when she walked in. "Why didn't they upgrade me to this suite? My agent asked if there were any suites open right before we sailed. That stupid—"

"They don't like to give away the perks that come with a suite. Sometimes they'd rather have it stand empty. Sit there," Catherine said firmly.

She and Bob escorted people to preassigned seats on the couches and added chairs. Along with Petronella and me, standing at one end of the lopsided oval, the idea was to break up the groups. The Valkyrie leader, the redhead, and the other one sat to Catherine's left. Then Constantine, Badar, and Pyorte before Bob separated them from Anya and Imka. Petronella came next, followed by Wardham, Maya, and Ralph.

Ralph was to my right. On my left were Odette, Coral, and Piper, then back to Catherine.

Next to the windows, bartender Jason offered non-alcoholic drinks from a wheeled cart. So far, no takers.

There were two more in the suite, but with the bedroom door nearly closed, no one could see Gerard Edgars or Henri Lipke.

"What is this about?" demanded the Valkyrie leader. Okay, I knew her name was Merilee—and a less appropriate name I couldn't imagine because there was nothing merry about her—but the Valkyrie leader suited her better. "We don't have all day."

"It's about murder. And finding the person guilty of murder."

"We didn't have anything to do with that old woman—sorry for your loss," she added in an unemotional monotone to Wardham before picking up in her usual delivery. "She went for a walk. Somebody knocked her off. This has nothing to do with us. I just came to check out the suite for our next cruise."

I talked over whatever response the redhead started to make, no doubt about who'd get the top suite.

"That's where you're wrong. It does have to do with you. Did you know some people consider members of your group prime suspects? Take for instance Petronella." Several of them looked around, homing in on her when she made a gulping sound of protest.

"She thinks Coral threatened Leah somehow and Leah tried to get her off the ship by tripping her on the stairs."

"What? That bitch? She tripped me?"

I hurried past Coral's questions undermining my premise. "She struck out with whatever she could at the moment. Her cane. She stuck it between the risers. Coral stepped on it and fell."

"I *knew* it wasn't my shoes." Coral's triumph wasn't pretty. "I kept saying it wasn't my shoes. I kept saying there was something wrong with the stairs."

"But it wasn't something wrong with the stairs. It was Leah's cane, which she put there on purpose. So it makes sense Coral went after Leah. She has the physical strength to kill Leah."

"What are you talking about? I don't know anything about how she was killed."

"As long as you asked, she was killed by something being pressed against her throat."

"How do you know that?" the Valkyrie leader asked.

"The experts will confirm it." I blithely committed them to my loosely woven suppositions. "Her cane was pressed against her throat while she was up against something unyielding, effectively strangling her."

Seeing all the other Valkyries, along with the rest of the people in the room looking at Coral gave me a little thrill.

It was working.

I could hardly believe it. I'd hoped, but hadn't truly believed. I wished Aunt Kit could be here.

I caught myself. This was barely the beginning and I was a newbie beyond all newbies at this.

Just as their suspicion stretched toward certainty, I cut it.

"The trouble is, Coral is the one person who couldn't have killed Leah."

"What?"

"Then why did you—?"

"What are you—?"

"Of course, I didn't."

I cut across all the voices "There is security footage."

The person who killed Leah already knew that, or they wouldn't have taken precautions to not be identifiable on the security footage.

"The reason we know Coral could not have been the killer is her cast would be instantly recognizable on the security video. Unless..."

I had everybody's attention.

"She could take off her cast."

"Well, I can't. So, you can just stop talking this crazy stuff."

"Oh, I've just started talking crazy stuff. Because there's a scenario with each of you as the murderer."

CHAPTER FORTY-THREE

THAT SHUT THEM up. The innocent trying to figure out what might look like guilt. The guilty reviewing every step taken to hide the trail.

"Now, let's consider, Anya and Pyorte," I said.

That set off babble. Possibly because most of them were relieved to hear someone else named.

"Who?" the redhead asked.

I tipped my head toward them. "They're musicians on the ship. They play guitar and violin."

"So?"

I turned away from her to the young duo. Both looked scared.

"It's time to be honest." I zeroed in on the violinist, her talented hands cupped in her lap, her fingertips twitching. "Why were you near Leah and Wardham's cabin not long before I found Leah?"

"Anya, you were near guest cabins? You know the rules." Pyorte sounded shocked, while overlooking the timing of her infraction.

She shook her head at him, mouth pressed firmly closed.

"It must have been important to break that rule." My nudge made no impression on her.

I went harder, keeping my voice and gaze even, relentless, the way I'd mastered when responding to the snarky minority of interviewers trying to get a cheap rise out of the author of *Abandon All*.

"You know there are cameras everywhere. When the officers check the video, they will see you by Leah Treusault's cabin. You must have been really angry at her, the way she chased after Pyorte. She made no secret of it. We all saw it. It was awkward and uncomfortable for anyone who noticed. But for you it was much more. If he gave in and got caught and fired, that would be the end of you playing together on the Diversion. What would you do then?"

It might have been a twitch, but I thought the head movement was a tiny, involuntary shake of her head, denying my words.

"But that was minor. There was so much more at stake. Because you love Pyorte and you were afraid... Such a rich lady. Would he be tempted? You went there to confront her."

"No, no." Thank heavens, I'd pushed her far enough to respond. I was running out of things to say. "You saw. I never stop there. You saw me. I thought... I did not stop there to hurt that woman."

True.

By then Leah was already dead, her body wrapped in towels and deposited on the deck chair.

"Why were you crying near her cabin? Crying so hard you almost ran into the wall."

"You catch me. I cry."

"You were already crying and I didn't catch you at anything. You weren't even by Leah and Wardham's cabin yet. What were you afraid of, Anya?"

"Nothing. Not afraid. No, no."

"Yes, you were. Afraid of—No, afraid *for*. You were afraid for Pyorte, weren't you?"

She burst into tears.

That worked as a yes for me.

Pyorte stretched a hand toward her, but with my arrangement couldn't reach her. "Anya, why?"

"You never come. All night. You are gone all night. Again."

Click. He got it. "You think I am with that woman? Anya, no. No."

Her tears started again.

This time when he reached, Bob gave me a questioning look. I nodded. He rose, Pyorte slid over immediately and put an arm around Anya, wiping at her tears, murmuring in their language. Bob took the empty chair.

This happened to the accompaniment of the redhead saying, "Big deal. The guy cheated on her. Doesn't have anything to do with us."

"Wait," I ordered before either of the ship officials—more likely Henri—could jump in to agree. "Your turn, Pyorte. Tell her why you were out all night."

He hesitated.

"C'mon. You and Badar. Can't you both see it's way past time to tell the truth. You've got Constantine tied up in this, while Anya and Imka are terrified for you two. There's been a murder. Badar is a suspect, now Pyorte will be too—if you don't tell the truth. This is not the time to worry about breaking a cruise line rule."

Badar broke in. "We didn't. It wasn't—"

"Pyorte?" Anya's eyebrows tipped up at the inner corners in pleading.

He slapped his hands on his thighs. "For the rings." Disappointment vibrated in the short words. "For *our* rings." He took her hand, his thumb rubbing over the ringless finger on her left hand. "To show the world."

"That you're married," I filled in.

He nodded, looking into Anya's eyes.

"But we agreed," she said, "our money, we save it."

"Not our money. *My* money I earn extra. I teach. Teach music."

She sucked in a breath. "The rules—"

"It's my fault. I asked him," Badar said. "I've been paying him to teach me to play the guitar and..." He looked toward Imka, then ground to a halt.

"Forget the surprise, forget breaking rules. Tell 'em." Constantine said. "*Murder.*"

"All right, all right. Yes. I wrote a song for your birthday." He threw the words at Imka. "A stupid song. And I got Pyorte to break the rules about extra jobs to teach me how to play it."

"Oh, Badar." She popped up and threw her arms around his neck and kissed him on the cheek. "A beautiful song."

"You haven't heard it."

"That is so," Pyorte said. "Song okay. Guitar not. Still."

"Hey—"

"I will love it. I do love it. My Badar." She half sat on Bob, who gently transferred her to Badar's lap.

So far, he was taking the brunt of this.

"Before you do any more kissing, let's get back to the murder. Though you *should* love that song, because it explains why Badar wouldn't give his alibi. He wouldn't expose Pyorte. How late were those two at it?" I directed that at Constantine.

"All night." He didn't sound happy. "It wasn't the first time. And there are some noises headphones don't cancel. Besides, try sleeping in headphones."

"He must practice. All time," Pyorte said.

"Imka's birthday is tomorrow." Badar's reward for knowing that was a huge, warm smile from her.

Then she turned it on me. "You know all this—how?"

I shrugged modestly. "Putting together a clue or two."

She regarded me with something like awe.

This wasn't awe for a book I hadn't written. This was for fashioning bits and scraps of looks and comments and timing to produce a conjecture. Not all that amazing, but mine, all mine.

Cutting across the warm fuzzies, the Valkyrie leader said, "You're tossing out names, then saying why they couldn't do it. If you know who the murderer is, just say so."

So much for awe.

She'd zeroed in on the weak point.

Because I didn't know. Not one hundred percent.

"It's called the process of elimination." And I needed these people to eliminate themselves. I didn't have enough information or time to do it for them. "Constantine, would you swear to it in court that Badar and Pyorte were in your cabin all that night."

"I would and so would the guys next to us. There, all night, playing that song over and over and over. Until Badar and I reported for work."

Why hadn't Edgars checked with the crew in nearby cabins? Or had he and already knew all this?

I pushed on.

"By that time security footage showed her body there for some time, when she would have been expected to be tucked up in her cabin sound asleep." I pivoted toward the widower. "But you say she wasn't."

"What? Oh ... Not in the cabin... No, she wasn't. Not when they came pounding on the door. I don't know about earlier. She could have come in, then left."

"Why would she?"

"She was an early riser."

"As early as four a.m.?"

"Well, uh, not usually. But she liked to get up, get things done, clear out the day." He sounded half asleep. Residual shock? How shocked could he be when he'd spent the night with Odette?

"What could she have been trying to clear out that day, Wardham?"

"I don't know. But with the longer days, she was getting up very early."

I looked to Maya and Ralph, then to Odette. "Did you know of anything she was doing that morning?"

They shook their heads.

"Anything that would draw her out of the cabin at that hour?"

More head shakes.

I looked at the Valkyrie leader. "You said she went for a walk."

"Hell, I don't know. I was just saying."

"She'd want her cane for a walk. But it can't be found now. Having the cane with her was her habit. True?"

This time, nods from Wardham, Odette, Ralph, and Maya.

"Let's consider other habits of hers."

"Like what?" Maya asked. Ralph touched her hand, perhaps in warning.

"She liked to know things about people."

Surprisingly, the response came from Wardham. "She did. She's been tracking some guy all over social media the past year. She said it made her a better bridge player to notice things about people. Especially their weaknesses."

Ralph and Maya shifted in their seats.

"Your group's cruised together for a long time. Until four years ago, when Maya was widowed by the death of her first husband, Bruce, during one of these transatlantic cruises."

That drew interested stares from the gathering except Wardham, Odette, and of course, Ralph, who covered her hand with his.

"I don't know what my first husband's death could possibly have to do with this horrible situation."

"That's what we're trying to find out. Leah and Ralph broke up on that same cruise. Leah and Wardham immediately became a couple. Then—" I looked around the room. "—Maya and Ralph got together."

They murmured, including something from the redhead about not knowing *they had it in them.*

I looked at Odette. "You likened it to a set of dominoes going down. But you were reluctant to say who toppled the first domino."

"My, you do remember things, Sheila Mackey." Her lips seemed to crackle with irritation even as they drew into a semblance of her smile. "And raise irrelevancies at the most inopportune time."

"It's a murder, Odette. Nothing is irrelevant. Inopportune is unimportant." I waited. She said nothing. "What started the chain of events on that cruise four years ago? Was it Bruce Froster's death? Did someone cause his death in order to bring about some part of that chain?"

Maya sucked in a breath. "Bruce?"

"No," Odette snapped, all astringent, no sweetness. "He died of natural causes. You want to hear this? Of course, Leah knocked over the first domino. I watched her. Tried to block her. But she held all the cards and full freedom to implement her strategy, since she had a dummy as a partner." In case that wasn't clear enough, she specified. "Wardham."

He winced. "But Odette..."

She turned on him. "But Odette, what, Wardham?"

"I thought you loved me. You invited me to your cabin. You slept with me. I mean..." He looked around without making eye contact, his cheeks growing ruddier, but a kind of pride there, too. "We had sex."

"We did have sex. I—"

"Wait a minute," I interrupted. "To be clear, you're talking about the night after Leah's body was found? Wardham did not spend that night in the cabin assigned to him while his was thoroughly searched and examined? Instead, he spent that night in your cabin?"

The Valkyries weren't bored now. Nobody was.

"Yes, he spent it with me. In my cabin." She said it like it was a technicality to get past. "I wanted to see if my memory was accurate. It was."

"Oh, Odette. You've missed me that much? I knew it. I broke your heart. I never should have left."

She stared at him a moment. "No, you shouldn't have. For your sake. I *did* love you. For decades. But I haven't loved you for years. Probably before you trotted off after Leah, certainly since. Having sex with you—and sleeping with you—confirmed my memory that it wasn't much to write home about. I've had better since we divorced. *Much* better."

"Odette! ... but then *why?*" he wailed.

She clicked her tongue and looked away from him.

"Yes, why?" I asked.

"To spit in Leah's eye one last time, of course. Even if she was dead, it was entirely satisfying. The night she died, the first night he was released from her bondage he came running back—" She smiled triumphantly. "—to me."

"WOULDN'T IT HAVE been more satisfying if she'd been alive?"

"Perhaps, but I couldn't be the cause of Wardham's murder." She made a sound, as if making a discovery. "I suppose I couldn't do it to Leah, either."

"Because you considered Leah a friend."

"Yes, yes, I did." She smiled slightly. "And didn't want to lose a good bridge partner."

"Odette, have you inherited a lot of money since you and Wardham divorced?"

"Me? No."

Her genuine surprise persuaded me.

Apparently it persuaded Petronella, too.

"You mean she didn't—? She's not the murderer? But then who...?" Hers cheeks turned dark red at letting it slip she'd thought Odette was the murderer.

I swung around to Maya.

"Maya, I, uh, happened to overhear you in town—in Santa Cruz—saying you knew about Leah's activities as Dee North. You were talking to Ralph about it in a little gift shop. I was back in a corner and couldn't help hearing you say you wanted her to know you knew." She looked blank. Not shock. Confusion. "That afternoon you did let her know, remember? You told her you knew she'd been posting nasty reviews as Dee North. But do you think anyone else knew or guessed or—?"

Lightning struck Maya, dispelling her confusion. I saw the flash the instant it happened.

"Oh, no, not Dee North. No, no, no." She shook her head and kept shaking it.

"But you did confront her. You told us all—" I tactfully skipped mentioning the dozens of other people at the pool she'd also informed. "—about Leah posting reviews as Dee North."

"Yes, *then*. But not earlier. In town I was talking to Ralph about something else entirely. Leah thought she was the only one who remembered, but I did, too."

"Remembered what?" I asked.

"The woman from two years ago." Maya turned to Imka. "Your friend, the girl who did my nails, told me what happened last year."

"What happened?" My heart hammered. Was this the break I'd told Edgars we might get?

"She'd been on this cruise two years ago with her husband, and he died during the cruise last year." She blinked suddenly teary eyes. Ralph put his arm around her. "Just like Bruce. Though not really like Bruce, because they were touring on land when he—"

"Another husband died?" Petronella interrupted, aghast.

"Two years ago?" I demanded at the same time. Then, more pertinently, "Which woman?"

But I knew.

"That woman." Maya pointed.

"Coral?" the Valkyrie leader asked.

"No. The woman now calling herself Piper." Without looking away, I asked Imka, "She called herself Laura another time, didn't she? Did she threaten you if you mentioned it?"

Imka nodded. "She was on the other ship where I worked, before I came here."

"Before she hooked up with a partner who made things so much easier for her to find prey for her black widow act. I heard someone talking about them a week before the murder, but only sorted it out today. Jason, who—*Security!*"

I might have intended to use Gerard Edgars' entire title, but there wasn't time. Jason jerked around, upsetting the drinks cart, jumping between two chairs and charging across the oval.

Petronella stood and flung out her arm, her elbow connecting with his nose, unbalancing him. He went over backward with a chair and Edgars scooped him up off the floor.

CHAPTER FORTY-FOUR

JASON WOULD HAVE been better off remaining where he was and trying to tough it out, as Piper did.

Where was he going? Even if he'd escaped the room, he couldn't get off the ship.

Blocked, he fell apart, crying and shouting it was all Piper. She'd killed the old woman. He'd known nothing about it until later.

What could Piper do except say, "I have no idea what you're talking about. He's lying. This is a big mistake. My husband will sue you all."

Henri Lipke led her out with a firm hold on her arm, nonetheless.

"What the hell? What the *hell*?" the Valkyrie leader said.

I faced the remaining four. "Did her husband's first wife recently inherit a lot of money?"

"Yeah, but... What the *hell*?" the leader repeated.

Turning to the redhead, I asked, "How did you know about the security cameras having gaps."

Piper's gasped *No* in response to the redhead saying there were cameras everywhere—and gaps in their coverage—had rung false. That might have been when she edged into my subconscious radar.

"Huh? Oh. From—" She bit it off.

No way was I letting that go. "Jason."

"That's not a crime. We talked. So what."

"I never liked her. Never." Coral's triumph was complete and oblivious to anything else. "But you said any one of us could've been the murderer. Not me. I can't take my cast off. You can't blame me."

"She already fingered Piper, you idiot," the Other One said.

With no hint of dismay, the redhead said, "Her husband's going to have a heart attack." Her expression changed. "*Hey*. She tried to hook me up with that Jason guy. A little fun, she said. Why that little—"

"Blackmail," the leader said with satisfaction.

The redhead lost all color. "I didn't do anything he could blackmail me for. Nothing. Ever."

"ACTUALLY," I TOLD Catherine, Bob, and Petronella after the others finally left, "I wouldn't be surprised if catching them now didn't prevent Piper's husband from having a heart attack in the near future, so Piper would inherit everything before he could dump her to go back to his previous wife."

Piper and Jason lived the crime I'd theorized for Maya and Ralph.

"But how did you know?"

"Imka's slip started it. Also her fellow nail tech said something about the cruise being cursed because, in addition to Leah, *she's back, too*. At first I thought she meant the Valkyrie leader." At their blank looks, I supplied, "Merilee. But I checked back with Bennie today and discovered Piper was on this cruise a year ago and she and Leah exchanged words. That might be what caught Leah's attention. She made sure to get the name of Piper's target a year ago, the man now Piper's husband."

"The social media Wardham mentioned?" Catherine asked.

"I suspect so. I'm sure the authorities will investigate. If so, it could easily have led her to Piper. I'd guess this year was supposed to be the payoff—Piper's downfall."

"Then why did she trip Coral?" Petronella asked.

"I'd bet she was trying to trip Piper. They were walking together. Coral stepped on the cane first. From Leah's viewpoint, it delivered the message she was someone for Piper to fear. But Piper ignored her—a smart reaction. That drove Leah nuts. She forgot caution in her zeal to make Piper see she knew what was going on and had the upper hand.

"Piper's current husband's good fortune was to be on the same cruises with Leah. A few frequent cruisers recognized Piper from other trips, including Maya. But none were interested enough—nosy enough—to put the pieces together."

"Or foolish enough to confront her," Bob said.

"True."

"How did you put this together?" Catherine asked.

"So many pieces. A lot of them eliminating other people. But one pointing to Piper was Imka referring to her as Laura the first day and Piper being far angrier at Imka than at Coral, who'd pushed her into the windows. All out of proportion. Plus, her overly shocked reaction to hearing one of the others say there were security cameras all over was off. Made me think she *did* know, which raised the question of how, which led to—"

"Jason," Catherine said.

"Exactly. Speaking of proportion, I almost eliminated her because I thought she was too tall to be the figure in the video. But that was wearing heels. She didn't wear them to carry Leah's body. No wonder she didn't look as tall. Without them she'd be about my height. Being out of her usual shoes also changed her walk.

"But the real clincher was Odette's friend—or acquaintance— Vance Reesha. I'd heard him gossiping with someone early on about a passenger who died in Rome last year. Then the widow picked up this cruise, *trolled* in the bars, and had a *new one* by the end of the cruise ... with some help. His listener asked something and he replied, *T-bar and errand chase sonar you and me theme and Cheese Mary now?*

"Oh, that clears it up," Bob said.

I grinned. "That's what I heard because of the wind and because I was falling asleep. Aunt Kit got me to take away the words and just listen to the sounds my memory stashed away. In other words, I'd mis-heard words and rather than record them as sounds, I'd created different words. When I went back to just the sounds, I finally could reconstruct the right words."

I did not tell them how the story in *The Fields of Athenry* got me thinking about couples and criminals. First, I connected Anya and Pyorte to the characters in the song. Then I took it another step and wondered about a couple committing far, far more serious crimes.

I looked around at them.

"*That bartender Jason. Or you mean the man she's married to now?* Hear it?" I repeated the nonsense words, then focused on just the sounds, before repeating what Vance actually said. "The significance was Jason helped Piper previously Laura and who knows what other names, troll for her next husband last year as soon as the previous one died in Rome."

Petronella's hands went to her mouth. "Oh, my goodness, do you think she killed that husband, too?"

"That," I said firmly, "is for the officials to find out."

CHAPTER FORTY-FIVE

THE THING ABOUT cruises is they end.

Our final day cruising.

Around the tip of Florida, then up its west coast through the waters of the Gulf of Mexico, and into Tampa at an inhumanly early hour. Thank heavens we didn't have to be off the ship then.

I had packing to do, but it could wait until after dark. For now, I'd enjoy the sun and the water.

After breakfast, of course.

Petronella was swarmed in the dining room. I felt a twinge of guilt to see her so overwhelmed.

Until she accepted one curious shipmate's handshake and murmured, "Oh, no, no, I couldn't possibly take *all* the credit."

Petronella was going to do just fine.

She was still talking with a large group, when I finished eating in peace. I gestured and mouthed that I would see her later.

I spent a leisurely morning at the pool.

I was leaning against the railing, waiting for Petronella to wrap up with two couples from Missouri expressing their admiration so we could have lunch, when Chief Security Officer Gerard Edgars settled in beside me.

"Your handiwork?" he asked with a nod toward Petronella. "Misleading the public?"

"You should talk. All that baloney about how Badar was being taken by authorities as soon as we docked in the Bahamas."

"No baloney employed. We never were to *dock* in the Bahamas, since we would have used the tender. It is a fine point, but a point nonetheless. One we discussed with both the Bahamian and American authorities. It was decided amongst us that the authorities in Tampa would be best equipped to handle such an investigation. As events transpired, we shall hand them a murderer and accessory."

"You *tricked* me.

"It was unconventional," he said smugly. "However, the circumstances called for it. You correctly stated that a number of people filled the requirements of motive, opportunity, and means. In addition to having familiarity with the guests from the days of the cruise, you were in a more advantageous position to question those people than we were and to hear whisperings we would never hear."

"Pretty sneaky."

"I believe you, too, employed a measure of stealth. I believe you did not share all you observed." He coughed delicately. "I asked if there was anything more. You said no, when there was. I considered how best to make use of whatever it was you were concealing."

"Very sneaky," I said admiringly. "You let me see the video on purpose, didn't you?"

He ignored the question, confirming my guess he'd wanted me to have that information without seeming to give it to me.

"Okay, but you have to tell me why Piper didn't throw the body overboard. Seems a lot simpler. I know they're developing technology to detect people going overboard, but the Diversion doesn't have it yet from what I read."

"It is well above my pay grade to confirm or deny what technology is employed. However, in the absence of such technology, there could yet be methods employing current technologies."

I thought a moment. "You have cameras trained along the railings to see if something or someone goes over? How many do you have? Do you cover the whole ship? Guest balconies? What about—?"

"Will not confirm or deny." His stern expression lightened. "However, one might say your interest in the whereabouts of Leah Treusault's cane led to a review which spotted a narrow object going overboard in a particular area now secured for the authorities in

Florida."

"You found the murder scene. Oh. The section of the deck you closed off."

"Alas, none of our cameras caught the crime." Another neither confirm nor deny. He cleared his throat. "Returning to the theme of sneaky, I am told the talk on the ship is how the murder was solved by your friend, Ms. Petronella Domterni."

"She deserves some time as the star." And the author of *Abandon All* didn't need the attention.

"No contradiction will come from those I command. However, I will need to convey accurately to the authorities how the information came to me."

I grimaced. I'd deal with that if I had to.

✧ ✧ ✧ ✧

LATE IN THE afternoon, I slowly pushed open the door for one final visit to the cozy spot beyond the indoor pool.

Odette sat in the middle deck chair, none of the others occupied.

I hesitated.

"Come sit, Sheila. Come sit."

I did. "Where are the others?"

"Ralph and Maya have been helping Wardham today with arrangements." Her mouth twisted. "They have the experience, since Ralph helped Maya when Bruce died. And I am giving Wardham space and time to adjust to the knowledge that I don't want him back."

She let out a long, slow breath.

"I don't know if we'll ever cruise together again. That's a shame, really, because I think we'd have a good time." She brightened. "Although maybe we will. Wardham will find someone quickly. He doesn't like being alone. And if we can guide him to the right sort... Oh, I see you're scandalized I might matchmake for my ex-husband. Left to his own devices, he'd be snapped up by one of the sort we've seen all too much of on this trip."

I wasn't totally sure if she meant Leah or the Valkyries. I agreed, either way.

"And I might find a companion suitable for a two-week cruise. As long as the others don't try to make it more. Perhaps a bridge player. Ah, there goes the sun."

We watched in silence as the orange and red circle sank below the horizon, while still splashing colors into the water and clouds.

"You know Leah was not like that when we met—the nastiness, the vicious reviews, hounding that poor boy who plays the guitar, the threats. Many bottles of wine become better with age. But a few turn to vinegar. Sometimes no one knows why."

Another silence fell between us.

She shivered. "It's chilly without the sun. I'd best go inside. Maya and Ralph and I are having room service together tonight. Don't want others to feel uncomfortable on this last night."

She gathered her things. We stood.

"Odette, you said the first day at the spa something about professionals and amateurs. What did you mean?"

"Oh…? Oh, yes." A small smile. "Those young women. The rivalries, the tangles, the emotions. That's what I meant. They made us look like amateurs."

Her smile softened and saddened. "Leah would never have believed she was tangling with someone tougher than her."

Odette gave me a quick hug and said, "Good luck to you, dear. And thank you."

I STOOD AT my balcony railing, watching the light of settlement, distant across the water, and the light of stars, even more distant.

The dining room had felt depleted. The remainder of the Valkyries and their "boys" sat at their usual table, but subdued beyond recognition. They never looked up from their plates. Except Coral, who stared at our table for a spell before tossing her hair and resuming her meal.

Petronella welcomed a flow of admirers. Catherine, Bob, and I chatted and I tried not to meet Catherine's eyes for too long because I'd start laughing.

It was a night of good-byes.

Eristo before dinner. Catherine and Bob, of course. Anya and Pyorte played in the Atrium—they'd never sounded better. They came over during a break, sharing their plans to buy rings, having decided they would be happy with what they could afford now. Imka and Badar slipped in, too. Badar had given her the birthday song last night. Scowling, he said he was awful. Smiling, she said he was magnificent.

Constantine, pressed into bartending service in Jason's absence, gave me two glasses of Veuve Clicquot and a wink with each. He was a much better winker than Jason.

He even gave a glass to Petronella.

She said, "Oh, no, I couldn't possibly." Then she drank it all.

One more sleep on the Diversion, then back to real life.

A new life.

My heart thudded harder against my ribs.

Anticipation, excitement, trepidation.

I was in my mid-thirties and I was ready—more than ready—to do something exotic.

Like move to the middle of the country and be normal.

No more interview queen. No more pretending I'd written something I hadn't. No more smiling past complaints about why didn't I write another *Abandon All*.

I think Aunt Kit had it right. One should be enough.

You know what? It *was* enough for me.

I was Sheila Mackey and outrageously fortunate that these fifteen years as someone else left me free now to be myself.

If another puzzle happened to come my way, I might just see what I could figure out.

I chuckled.

I'd be a sleuth with a secret.

Oh.

Yes, yes, yes. And I wanted a dog.

A sleuth with a secret and a big, furry dog.

And a better Doctor Watson than Petronella, bless her heart. What were the chances I could persuade Catherine and Bob to leave

Scotland?

It wasn't a whole plan for the rest of my life, but it was the beginning of one.

I liked it.

The End

Enjoy **Death on the Diversion**? (Hope so)

Sheila, Kit and friends ask if you'll help spread the word about them and the new Secret Sleuth series. You have the power to do that in two quick ways:

Recommend the book and the series to your friends and/or the whole wide world on social media. Shouting from rooftops is particularly appreciated.

Review the book. Take a few minutes to write an honest review and it can make a huge difference. As you likely know, it's the single best way for your fellow readers to find books they'll enjoy, too.

To me—as an author and a reader—the goal is always to find a good author-reader match. By sharing your reading experience through recommendations and reviews, you become a vital matchmaker. ☺

For news about upcoming Secret Sleuth books, as well as other titles and news, join Patricia McLinn's Readers List and receive her twice-monthly free newsletter.
www.patriciamclinn.com/readers-list

Other Secret Sleuth cozy mysteries

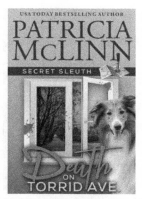

DEATH ON TORRID AVE.
A new love (canine), an ex-cop and a dog park discovery.

DEATH ON BEGUILING WAY
Sheila untangles the untimely death of a yoga instructor.

DEATH ON COVERT CIRCLE

"[Death on the Diversion] is such an enjoyable story, reminiscent of Agatha Christie's style, with a good study of human nature and plenty of humor. Great start to a new series!"

—5-star review

"[Death on Torrid Avenue] is told with a lot of humor and the characters are good company. I thoroughly enjoyed myself and am looking forward to the next story."

—5-star review

Caught Dead in Wyoming mysteries

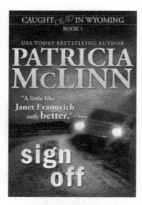

SIGN OFF

Divorce a husband, lose a career ... grapple with a murder.

LEFT HANGING

Trampled by bulls—an accident? Elizabeth, Mike and friends must dig into the world of rodeo.

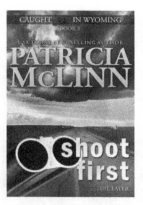

SHOOT FIRST

For Elizabeth, death hits close to home. She and friends must delve into old Wyoming treasures and secrets to save lives.

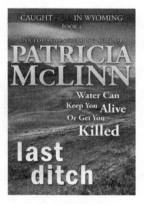

LAST DITCH

KWMT's Elizabeth and Mike search after a man in a wheelchair goes missing in dangerous, desolate country.

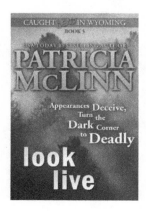

LOOK LIVE

Elizabeth and friends take on misleading murder with help—and hindrance—from intriguing out-of-towners.

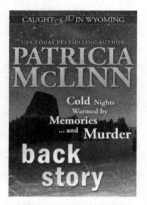

BACK STORY

Murder never dies, but comes back to threaten Elizabeth, her friends and KWMT colleagues.

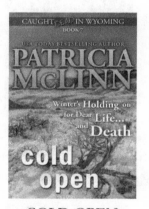

COLD OPEN

Elizabeth's looking for a place of her own becomes an open house for murder.

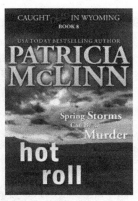

HOT ROLL

Death on a tight deadline for Elizabeth and the investigative team.

REACTION SHOT

"While the mystery itself is twisty-turny and thoroughly engaging, it's the smart and witty writing that I loved the best."

—Diane Chamberlain, New York Times bestselling author

"Colorful characters, intriguing, intelligent mystery, plus the state of Wyoming leaping off every page."

—Emilie Richards, USA Today bestselling author

Mystery With Romance

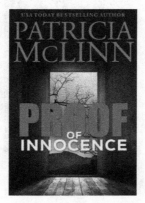

PROOF OF INNOCENCE

She's a prosecutor chasing demons. He's wrestling them. Will they find proof of innocence?

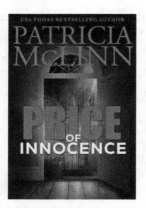

PRICE OF INNOCENCE

She runs a foundation dedicated to forgiveness. He runs down criminals. If they don't work together, people will die.

"Evocative description, vivid characterization, and lots of twists and turns."

—5-star review

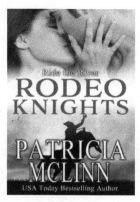

RIDE THE RIVER: RODEO KNIGHTS

Her rodeo cowboy ex is back … as her prime suspect.

BARDVILLE, WYOMING

A Stranger in the Family

A Stranger to Love

The Rancher Meets His Match

Explore a complete list of all Patricia's books

www.patriciamclinn.com/patricias-books

Or get a printable booklist

patriciamclinn.com/patricias-books/printable-booklist

New! Patricia's eBookstore (buy digital books online directly from Patricia)

patriciamclinn.com/patricias-books/ebookstore

About the Author

USA Today bestselling author Patricia McLinn spent more than 20 years as an editor at the Washington Post after stints as a sports writer (Rockford, Ill.) and assistant sports editor (Charlotte, N.C.). She received BA and MSJ degrees from Northwestern University.

McLinn is the author of more than 50 published novels, which are cited by readers and reviewers for wit and vivid characterization. Her books include mysteries, romantic suspense, contemporary romance, historical romance and women's fiction. They have topped bestseller lists and won numerous awards.

She has spoken about writing from Melbourne, Australia, to Washington, D.C., including being a guest speaker at the Smithsonian Institution.

Now living in northern Kentucky, McLinn loves to hear from readers through her website, Facebook and Twitter.

Visit with Patricia:

Website: https://www.patriciamclinn.com

Facebook: facebook.com/PatriciaMcLinn

Twitter: @PatriciaMcLinn

Pinterest: pinterest.com/patriciamclinn

Instagram: instagram.com/patriciamclinnauthor

CPSIA information can be obtained
at www.ICGtesting.com
Printed in the USA
LVHW090853051220
673420LV00039B/789